Aella Greene

John Peters

Vol. II.

Aella Greene

John Peters
Vol. II.

ISBN/EAN: 9783337041373

Printed in Europe, USA, Canada, Australia, Japan

Cover: Foto ©Andreas Hilbeck / pixelio.de

More available books at **www.hansebooks.com**

VOLUME II.

By AELLA GREENE,

AUTHOR OF "WHERE THE NOBLE HAVE THEIR COUNTRY,"
"STANZA AND SEQUEL" AND OTHER POEMS.

PUBLISHED IN 1891.

CONTENTS.

JOHN PETERS.
II.

CHAPTER I.

"THE PROPER PAPERS."

INTENTLY watching the boy for a few moments longer, the doctor responded to Elder Peters: "There must be something in your idea, and how fortunate was your coming! A possibility of restoring the sufferer—let us improve it. Cruelty has crushed him—kindness is the antidote. In one so young nature will bring a reaction of the benumbed physical powers and a reviving of spirits, the awakening from the night of despair to the dawn of hope! The crisis will be then. Let the first object on which rest the opening eyes be the face of some one who has been friendly to him. And let that face show calmness and sincerity, melt with tenderness and glow with sympathy! Let there be no crossing of the enfeebled will in the attempts to assert itself, whatever those attempts are. And let the hand of genuine interest and love be extended to lead the will up the steep to the summit of assurance, where it shall breathe in, from the genial air of verity, the consciousness of the right to be. If those first attempts show only the will power of an infant, then, while bestowing on the boy the tenderness befitting the care of a babe, regard him—and show that regard—regard him with the respect due to one who has endured that which would demand the fortitude of a full-grown man."

Dr. Johnson, whose words had been spoken in tones scarcely above a whisper, concluded with this question to Mrs. Sumner: "You have been kind to the boy—have you not?"

"I have tried to be."

"Have you been kind to him? Speak without fearing that you will be thought egotistic in telling, in this emergency, your kindness."

"Thank God, I have been kind to Edward."

"Sit by him—there, he opens his eyes, see—"

And the bewildered gaze of the boy spoke the feeble attempts of the will to reassert itself, efforts which a breath of opposition would have baffled to the blotting out of the power to repeat them, power that might have been overcome also by the delirium of joy caused by a too sudden announcement of all the good in store for the sufferer. To the question she divined in his eyes, the motherly woman who knelt at the couch replied:—

"Yes, Edward, it is Mrs. Sumner."

"How did you get into the barn?"

"Why, Edward, you are in Mr. Sumner's house."

"I'm so glad—who brought me here?"

"Mr. Sumner and Elder Peters."

There was a look of assurance on Edward's face as he sank back on his pillow for a few moments; when, his eyes again opening, Mrs. Sumner continued:—

"Here, too, are Mr. Edgerley and Mr. Stedman ; and Dr. Johnson has come up from Dayville to help you get well again. So, my brave little man, have good courage."

"Yes, Mrs. Sumner"—and warm tears coursed down the cheeks of the boy, at sight of which the doctor exclaimed, "Thank God, there is hope now. And," continued he, stooping by the couch, "now let me look at your back."

"Yes, sir ; you may, but it is very sore."

"All right, my little man, I'll hurt you as little as possible."

When Elder Peters had lowered the boy's clothing,— "O, my God !" exclaimed the physician, "one, two, three, four, five,"—and the count of blows ran up to twenty-five, with welts indicating previous scourgings ! And Dr. Johnson continued, "O, my God ! a child innocent as a sunbeam suffering a punishment that only the lower grades of civilization allow to be inflicted on adult criminals ! What monsters they, who, professing the name of Christ, and claiming to be par excellence Christian, partake, in this day of the Christian era, so fully the spirit of the Herod who destroyed the infants that he might in the slaughter include the infant founder of the gospel of peace and good will ! Gracious Heaven, spare the life and the reason of this one of the Father's little ones !"

These words of imploration ended, Elder Peters, on his knees, and reverently looking upward, offered this expressive petition :—

"And if possible, for the sake of Him who, on the cross, forgave the thief, do Thou, O, God, forgive the perpetrator of this damning crime to which the Book affixes the penalty of the mill-stone and the depths of the sea as a leniency of infliction !"

Fearing that Grout might come to demand the surrender of the boy, and correctly thinking that the very sight of the tyrant would drive him mad, Dr. Johnson directed that he be carried to a chamber where he would be at one more remove from intruders.   His raw back washed with warm water and bathed with tincture of myrrh that made the flesh smart intensely for a few moments, with the soothing effect that followed, the boy, whispering, "That feels so good," sank into a sweet slumber, carrying with him the consciousness that Timothy Edgerley sentineled his rest.

The wound in Stedman's face, which proved to be a very severe one, next received the attention of the doctor, who, that duty done, said :—

"Now my fleet and faithful 'Flyer'—I must see him. It was a terrible drive he made."

Returning from the barn where the horse had been carefully groomed, blanketed and fed, the doctor said :—

"As I feared, fevered feet and chest—and a foundered horse.   But the sacrifice was made in a good cause.   And there is hope for 'Flyer' yet."

A veterinary living in the neighborhood was summoned and given instructions to do his best, when Dr. Johnson, returning again to the house, said :—

"I would retire did not something tell me there may be another scene in the drama of the day, and one in which I may be wanted."

"Dr. Johnson," said Elder Peters, "you do well to heed the leadings of the Spirit."

Justice Houston of Hardland was judicial. He had long held the opinion that Grout's cruelty unfitted him for being master of the boy, but had not expressed that opinion to any one. When Grout, on the day of the capture, applied to the magistrate for authority to compel Edward's rescuers to surrender him, the justice replied, without hint, by word or look, of his real opinion :—

"I'll issue the proper papers in the case and will personally place them in the hands of Officer Newton, who will accompany you as you go to demand the surrender of the boy."

And Deacon David Grout, as he returned from Houston's, said to himself, "I'll have the reprobate and teach those New Lights not to meddle with my affairs."

Deputy Sheriff Charles Newton of Hardland could be uncommunicative. And he said little as he walked with Deacon Grout to Sumner's house. He knew that, to men not blinded by their own self-importance as was Grout, his silence would have been suspicious. But Deacon Grout dreamed not of the dénouement of defeat awaiting him through the instrumentality of the men of the law, who, ·of course, would be in accord with a representative of the gospel like himself!

At the suggestion of the officer, who entered the side door to have a conference with Mrs. Sumner, Grout rapped at the front door, which was opened by Dr. Johnson. That gentleman's professional protest against Grout's design, as sure to turn Edward insane, was spurned by the egotistic "foreordained," who thrice demanded the surrender of the boy, and called on Officer Newton to take him.

Having in his make-up the spice of a liking for mischief, and so wishing to protract the drama that was being enacted, Newton counseled against "haste in the matter."

But the officer, who kept his own plans from the deacon, was himself ignorant of the plans of the latter, who now retired, and in such a manner as to arouse in Newton the expectation of some new development, that would increase the complications and make more difficult of execution the plan to the carrying out of which he was committed in the name of justice, and by a promise to the magistrate, who had issued the papers for him to serve. Returning, soon after, with Deacon Granger, Nathan Lyman and Calvin Clough, Deacon Grout introduced them as " brethren in good and regular standing in the church, who have come to help me take the boy and as witnesses to my promise to treat him better."

The first visit of Grout awakened Edward, and he shook with apprehension at the voice of the tyrant, as he heard it from his chamber. But he was reassured to calmness by this utterance from one whom he knew meant exactly what he said, and was fully able to do all he promised :—

"Little feller, it's Tim Edgerley thet's by ye, an' naow don't ye be afeard o' anythin' thet Grout kin do to ye. He'll never lay his hands on Edward Atherton agin, or I'm not Tim Edgerley from Noo Hampshear."

"O, that's so good! And Mr. Edgerley, you'll stay right here, won't you?"

"Yis, my little feller, an' Tim Edgerley's bound to back up his promise thet no Grout kin step inside o' this room," and the giant laid his great hand tenderly on the boy's head—"rest naow, for yer jest as safe as ef yer own father was here a-talkin' to ye."

"O, papa, papa, why was you killed! Papa, papa—"

"My little feller, God bless ye. Tim Edgerley's yer friend, from this aout, and don't yer be cryin' tew much. Jest rest, an' ye'll get over this, an' there's somethin' tells me ye'll have a happy life."

The boy lay back on his couch and closed his eyes.

At Newton's suggestion Mrs. Sumner, as mistress of the house, ordered Grout to leave, and with his refusal at the second request, he demanded that "Newton proceed according to the papers given him by Justice Houston."

"That I will," said the officer; "one commands me to arrest you for trespass in the event of your refusing to leave the premises, as you have twice been ordered to do."

"What, a conspiracy!" exclaimed Grout, advancing

as if to mount the door-step and shaking a fist at the officer.

"Violence will do no good.   Justice Houston promised you to 'issue the *proper papers*,' and I think he has so done.   Another of the precepts commands your arrest for assault, if you intimidate any people who are rightfully here.   For what you have already done I could arrest you on the two charges I have mentioned; but if you leave at once all will be well."

The officer increased his earnestness of command as he heard through the open door of the chamber the boy's whispered words of dread and Edgerley's assuring "Little feller, they'll not let him git inside the house, an' Tim Edgerley kin drop a dozen like Grout tryin' to git in here."

Grout did not recede, but declared, "I'll have him;" whereat, on the preconcerted signal of a low whistle, Mr. Peters left his place by Stedman and went up to comfort and guard Edward, and the tall form of the "Noo Hamp-shear" man descended the stairs, and the officer said, "Mr. Edgerley and Dr. Johnson, exercising the right which the law gives me of deputizing as many assistants as an emergency renders necessary, I appoint you to help me, and those men must leave at once!"

There was a relishable readiness of manner in the giant's movements, as, laying his hand gently on Dr. Johnson's shoulder to assure him that he alone was equal to the occasion, he said, striding toward the besieging quartette :—

"Fellers, yer room's better'n yer company. Marvil tew wunst!"

But they heeded him not; and, seconding words with action, the giant grasped Grout by the coat collar and the nether garments, and, in spite of a vigorous resistance, lifted him over the fence and seated him gently on the turf by the road-side, saying, as he deposited the helpless man, "Dave Grout, ye must be gittin' tired; I'm anxious fur yer health, an' advise ye to rest a while."

Deacon Granger, protesting in an irate manner against Edgerley's feat, did not have time to finish his wrathful demurrer before he found himself seated by the side of his brother deacon, where, to complete the row, the giant landed Lyman and Clough. Though not in the least harming the besiegers, Edgerley was so convincing in his manner of "setting them down" that, when landed, they dared not move. When he had deposited the last of the four he leisurely stepped into the road and said, as he looked patronizingly down on them :—

"Fellers, be good boys and ye kin go home bimeby," concluding his remarks with this bit of irony, suggested by their abject position, "I thought ye belonged tew *the stan'in' committee.*"

Entertained with the sport that Edgerley made of clearing the premises, Newton went out to the road, and, at his suggestion, the giant said, "Fellers, make yerselves skace, an' never come agin."

"There," said Edgerley to the boy, when relieving Mr.

Peters as sentinel of the sufferer, "little feller, Ole Grout an' them what come tew help him were mighty glad ter budge, an' they'll never come agin."

After the laugh at Edgerley's novel behavior, Dr. Johnson again visited his horse, and, returning to the house and giving his patients another look, sought the chamber assigned him and slept soundly. His full health was equal to the excitement of an emergency like that in which he had acted, while he found cheer in the consciousness that he was at work in the cause of humanity, that he was succeeding in his undertakings and that he was appreciated for what he had done. Kneeling by the side of Stedman, Elder Peters thanked God for the happy issue vouchsafed their novel mission, and, disposing himself for the night on the couch improvised for him, close at hand, and filled with the thoughts of the wonderful way God had led him, he was soon lulled to rest by the murmur of voices in the living-room. There Mary Sumner, who had always been on good terms with Mr. Newton, kept him company as he tarried to guard the house, and was rejoiced to read unmistakable evidence in his manner that his liking for her was on the increase, while, of course she pitied her friend Huldah Grout who was her rival for Newton's hand. Miss Grout was a worthy young woman, and, partaking largely the nature of her mother, that contained the elements of tenderness and justice, was naturally opposed to her father's abuse of the boy, against which she had protested, reaching the climax of her objections on

the return from the defeated attempt to recapture
Edward :—

"There, father, that cruel whipping you gave Edward
will make everybody hate you and—" she did not say as
she thought, "you have spoiled my chances with Mr.
Newton," but did say, after a moment's pause, "I shan't
blame Mary Sumner half as much as I do you."

Edgerley, from the north window of the chamber, gazed
off towards ——, the home of Jennie Davis! And then,
tucking in the "little feller" whom he delighted to be-
friend, he stretched his gigantic frame among the blankets
and pillows which Mrs. Sumner had placed at his disposal
on the carpet, and was soon sleeping as sweetly as he
would if lulled by the ripple of the brooks that sang their
merry course toward the joyous Ammonoosuc.

In the morning the doctor found his patients improving
and saw that the veterinary intrusted with the care of
"Flyer" was doing well for the horse. Writing and posting a letter to "Andrew M. Harrison, Esquire, Wayfield,"
he gave directions for the care of Mr. Stedman and
Edward and positive orders that under no circumstances
should Grout be allowed to see the boy or the latter be
left in fear of molestation by the tyrant, and, procuring
the best driver and fleetest horse the livery of the village
afforded, was soon bounding along the road toward Dayville. Two days later Elder Peters, who had so won by
his love and tenderness on Edward's heart that the boy
forgave Grout for his cruelty and actually prayed for

God's blessing on the man, started homeward with his
protégé whom he meditated keeping under his own care
until a place should be provided for him. The fine
scenery of the route, the music of birds and brooks that
made melodious the flower-scented air of the bright June
morning, and the consciousness that he had done his duty
and found his undertaking crowned with signal success,
filled his heart with gratitude and joy, and no wonder
that he burst forth singing,

"Come, Thou Fount of every blessing!"

And Edward Atherton, five years to a day from the
time when, by a standing order religionist, he was con-
signed to servitude under one of the foreordained unto
eternal salvation, was carried by a New Light preacher
to be provided with a good home among those who held
that "whosoever will" may be saved, those who believed
God to be not only the Ruler of the Universe but the
Great Father of humanity, those who believed in the
Apostles' creed rather than in the dread "decrees," those
who had read not only the seventh chapter of Romans, but
the eighth, those who held that afflictions are not always
judgments sent as punishments for sin, but are sent as
medicine from the Great Physician. Does it need to be
asked whether or not Edward Atherton became a New
Light? Does it need to be asked if Elder Peters believed
more than ever in heeding the voice within? And is it a
wonder that when all the circumstances of the rescue of

Edward Atherton became known to Rev. Dr. Robinson he exclaimed with a heartiness that would have satisfied the New Lights themselves, "Thank God, Brother Peters! and that is a beautiful idea of yours about following the leadings of the Spirit. It has worked a marvel in the case of the boy, and I find much Scriptural authority for it."

"Murderous! Damnable!" exclaimed Mr. Harrison, as, handing to his law partner a letter from Dr. Johnson, he began writing as a man does who is in earnest.

"Out-Heroding Herod!" responded Mr. Jameson, "and I hope you will do your best to bring the monster to justice!"

"The first thing to be done is to break Grout's legal hold on the boy."

It goes without saying that, at the hearing on the petition for the annulling of the indenture of Edward Atherton to David Grout, Mr. Harrison took good care of the case intrusted to him by Dr. Johnson, and that, the testimonies of that gentleman, Mr. Sumner, Elder Peters, and Timothy Edgerley made it clear that the ends of justice could be served only by granting the petition. Grout had been summoned to "show cause" why the petition should not be granted, but, failing to respond, he forfeited his right of appeal from the decision in favor of the petition; and when Officer Newton, armed with an order of court, appeared to demand the "instrument of indenture and any and all effects belonging to the said Edward Atherton that are in the possession of David Grout aforesaid," the "aforesaid David" reluctantly proceeded to comply with the request, and Huldah Grout said when the officer departed, "There, father, what did I tell you?"

Does any one ask, what did Mrs. Mehetabel Simpkins Atherton think about the boy? What had she thought about him at any time during the five years "sence he was baound aout ter Dekin Graout's?" He was off her hands, so she would not have to support him, and was where he would be "made ter stan' raoun'," and she was satisfied! When, just for the "name on't," she went up to see him at Hardland, she came back delighted with the fact that when he "went ter showin' sum o' his Atherton high noshins, Dekin Graout tuck 'em outen him with er ox gad." And when she learned that he had been taken from Grout's keeping her first fear was that she would be obliged to support him, and her second was that he would not be "made ter mind." But, assured by Mrs. Smith, by whom she had been invited to tea when the boy was to be absent with Elder Peters, that she, Mrs. Mehetabel Simpkins Atherton, would not be in the least responsible for Edward's board and clothes, and that she, the speaker, would see that the boy was "taught to obey," Mrs. Mehetabel declared her "consarn was clean gone," and she readily signed a petition for the appointment of Daniel and Elizabeth Smith as guardians of Edward Atherton.

"Capital management," said Esquire Harrison, as giving Mr. Smith the document appointing himself and Mrs. Smith, he drew from Mr. Smith the account of his wife's shrewdness in dealing with Mrs. Atherton! "capital management! and fortunate indeed is it for the boy that he is protégé of such wise and humane people as the Smiths of Dayville. The further proper papers would be those commanding the arrest of the accursed Grout for his cruelties! But I suppose that, copying the Christ-like Elder Peters, you will forgive the Herod of Hardland!"

Calling on her friends shortly after their appointment, Mrs. Taylor was thus addressed by Mrs. Smith when the two were alone : "Tell me, why was it that Edward inherited all his father's good qualities and almost absolutely nothing of the cheapness and meanness of the one who was mother of his physical self?"

"Well I do not know the reason, but I remember that when Mr. Taylor told me that Atherton expected to become a father I thought to ask Samuel to tell Atherton to be sure and be kind to his wife, even if she had been unkind to him ; and I knew she had. And Mr. Taylor is real good to understand things, and he went straight up to Atherton's and did the errand in good earnest. And three years after, when I saw Atherton with the boy and the little fellow happy with him, I thought and—thought ! "

"How beautiful your act! how timely, how important!

And the results of it shall last and increase through time and blossom in eternity!" The two women, hand in hand, thrilled with thoughts that were beyond the power of utterance!

"How beautiful, how grand!" continued Mrs. Smith, as she arose and left the room. Returning soon after with the boy, she said:—"Edward, this is Mrs. Taylor, who has loved you for years, and who has lost her own son and wants some one to take his place."

"Mrs. Taylor—Mrs. Taylor," responded the boy, meditatively, "yes, my father used to know Mr. and Mrs. Taylor."

When, the next day, Edward Atherton knocked for admission to the house of the "honest miller," he carried a note which ran:—

DAYVILLE, June—, 1855.

DEAR MRS. TAYLOR:

In the good providence of Him who doeth all things well it has been ordered that I have the legal right to say that which my feelings prompt me to speak and which my judgment approves—take to your home and your heart one whom your thoughtfulness blessed before his breath began. I shall rejoice to see him the recipient of your affection and giving, in return, the respect and love which your kindness will call forth. Love him so much that it will be his ambition to please you by a right life. Mr. Smith and myself will want to see him every week, and send him to us, attended by angels that your faithful prayers shall summon to guard his steps. Congratulating you on having a child to love and asking you to remember, and to pray that I remember, that, there is on earth no nobler mission than ministering to the little ones, I am

Always your friend,

ELIZABETH SMITH.

CHAPTER II.

THE attention demanded by his own concerns, the
post-office and the increasing business of the growing town, not leaving Mr. Smith time to care prop-
erly for the interests of the new corporation, Mr. Stedman
was intrusted with their enterprise, and as soon as he had
sufficiently recovered from his injuries to admit of the
activity, he began superintending the workmen engaged
in building the mill, of which, when completed, the next
year, he was made manager and charged with hiring help,
purchasing stock, and marketing the product. This position, whose duties called him occasionally to New York
and Boston, gave him opportunity for outlook into the
business world ; his acquaintance with Mr. Harrison was
a source of social influence, and accepting that gentleman's invitation to speak in the first national campaign of
the Republicans, he appeared on the platform with Anson
Burlingame, Charles Sumner, and other eloquent expo-
nents of the principles of that party, and made telling addresses in advocacy of John Charles Fremont, the Path-
finder of Empire, for the presidency. And, wholly innocent of the full scope of Mr. Harrison's plan in calling

him into the field, he found himself, through that gentleman's seeking, elected to the Legislature in opposition to
Lemuel Barnes, once selectman of Dayville, and now and
evermore chief of the Dayville foreordained and elected
unto salvation, and so, of course, entitled to an election
to the Legislature! Chagrined at his defeat by one so
wholly unworthy his steel as a New Light, and jealous at
the evident popularity of Stedman, Barnes vowed ven-
geance on the man, and found comfort in the sympathy of
the Reverend Jonathan Edwards Barber, who thought
anything right that was damaging to the New Lights, because that which hindered them advanced the cause of
sound doctrine; who, as it proved, thought that even the
machinations of a slanderer were chosen of God to rebuke
those holding unsound doctrines!

Of course New England, which has undoubtedly shared
in the "improved condition of mankind" of which the opti-
mists tell, now has few, if any, of those who, never thrilling with noble impulses themselves, suppose others incapable of them; few who see a tinge of foolishness, if not
an element of actual sin, in the highest and manliest gal-
lantries that charm woman's heart and inspire the fit re-
ciprocaticn. But the average typical town of old time
New England contained representatives of that class.
And generally, the fewer the people, the more numerous
in proportion were these evil-eyed ones; and the shal-
lower the social life of the place, the busier were they in
voicing their surmisings. And Dayville was no exception.

to this rule, for there dwelt Sam Simpkins, senior, who in his prime excelled all others in the manufacture of scandals.

With his increasing years the people had a respite from the Simpkins venom, but his son, Sam Simpkins, junior, who had in his father's time tried his tongue at the bad business, took on an ambition at his father's death to maintain the reputation of the family for destroying reputations. Prompted by his greed for making people suffer, and in keeping with a long cherished wish to "get even" with Mr. Stedman, for being compelled to pay him a just claim, he started stories against him and Mrs. Wilcutt, in 1857, which grew from molehills of fancy to mountains of fact, and which, at the suggestion of Mr. Barnes were brought by Mr. Cheatham, the prosecuting attorney for the district, to the attention of the grand jury. Importuned by him, they "found probable cause" and reported a "true bill," of which Stedman learned through an officer who apprehended him and required him to give bail for his appearance for trial, the next week, adding, "It's the hardest duty I ever had to do."

"That was Deputy Sheriff Cushman," said Mr. Harrison to Stedman, when the latter came to tell what happened and engage the lawyer to defend him, "and well he might regret being charged to arrest Thomas Stedman, one who is the soul of honor, one whose acquaintance is creditable to any lady who has it, and one whose acquittal I'll secure, or my name is not Andrew M. Harrison!" And the jurist emphasized his indignation at the injustice of the finding, by a vigorous blow on his office table, and said to his partner, "Mr. Jameson, attend to all other matters committed to us and give me what assistance you can in this case. By the way, who is to preside this term?"

"Judge Robinson, cousin of the Wayfield divine."

"Capital! he's not only a good judge, but a sensible man; one with whom justice is more than law, and with whom law is nothing unless it is just."

At the opening of the cases of "the Commonwealth versus Thomas Stedman; same versus Mary Wilcutt," the place of trial was filled with the best people of Wayfield and vicinity, who came to manifest their interest in the proceedings and their belief that the result would show Mr. Stedman and the lady implicated to be wholly innocent of the charges made against them in the name of justice, but, as Mr. Harrison said in presenting the case, "really brought to gratify the greed of a Simpkins, punish the successful political rival of Lemuel Barnes, and damage those opposed to the cast-iron creed of the Reverend Jonathan Edwards Barber!"

A certificate of Dr. Johnson to the effect that Mrs. Wilcutt was so unnerved by the accusation that compelling her attendance at court would cause insanity, was reluctantly accepted by the prosecution, and the trial began with only one of the defendants in attendance. In accepting this arrangement there should have been no hesitancy, the other party accused being on bail with ample sureties, and trying and acquitting one defendant tried and acquitted the other, and trying and condemning one defendant tried and condemned the other.

In his vigorous but fair cross-questioning of the witnesses against his clients, Mr. Harrison occasionally dealt a master stroke with his blade of irony that riddled into shreds the testimony detailing the attentions of Mr. Stedman to his friend—his drives with her, his loitering strolls with her by moonlight, his affectionate caresses at parting at her door, and, "climax of impropriety and sure evidence of sin! his tarrying with her in a tenantless house for shelter from a terrific storm that overtook them on their return from calling at the home of a friend! Proof positive of wrong-doing seen by the redoubtable Simpkins himself! Unbeknown to his victims he lurked in the chamber of the house to watch them on their walk and from his perch observe what he might, had not this god-send of a storm come to stamp the scheme of a sneak with the sanction of the skies!"

To show the estimation in which good people held the defendants, "who needed no vouching," Mr. Harrison introduced Rev. Dr. Robinson, Deacon Sherwood and Mr. Smith—whose opinions of the accused Mr. Cheatham did not see fit to controvert—and came to his argument with the calmness of a man conscious but not vain of the ability to do the work before him :—

"May it please the Court; Mr. Foreman and Gentlemen:—Confessing my inability to invest such evidence with significance enough to merit the ridicule of respectable people, I shall offer nothing in refutation of the flimsy and shadowy pretense of proof given by the prosecution in support of the fabrication of a slanderous Simpkins, which the government, through the procuring of a disappointed politician and a bigoted theologian, has brought to damage the good name of the manliest man I ever met, and a lady of whom I say,

> 'Some angel guide my pencil while I draw
> What nothing else than angel can excel!'

And I fearlessly place in your hands their deserved reputations for excellence as outweighing all the accusations made by the instigators of these proceedings, for the origin of which wickedness one would naturally look to the fiends of whom the theologies tell! But, if, with the worst machination possible for them to invent, the most daring of their number had come to earth to seek a human agent to whom to intrust the launching of the falsehood, and had ventured before Simpkins, that fiend would have trembled in the presence of such superiority of malignity, where, if he could endure until the slanderer had told his own design, the devil would have cried out in protest of pity at thought of the intensity of evil which the lie concocted by Simpkins would work, and finding his dissuasives of no avail, he would have fled in glad haste to the better society of devils damned! This, gentlemen, is the fabrication you are asked to consider; this the companionship, spurned of fiends, to which you are invited!

"Tracing backward one generation the line of the chief slanderers of this region we come to the elder Simpkins, whose venom some of the victims survived. Two of them perished; and to this day reference to their untimely death brings a shudder of dread. Agnes Stuart, as good and lovely a woman as ever came, kissed by the airs of the heather hills of her native Scotland, to bless an American in his own clime, was one of these victims; and by her side, the star blotted from his sky, the sun extinguished in his heaven! they soon laid the form of the manly Ralph Jameson! After brief release from such infliction, the people are again put in dread of a Simpkins, and one ambitious to outdo the wickedness of his predecessor and sire!

"Mr. Foreman and Gentlemen—I shall ask no excuse for earnestness on this occasion. Indeed, were I indifferent, the very walls of this temple of justice would cry out against the cowardly silence over that wrong-doing for which not only the English language confesses itself at fault in lacking the words of fit denunciation, but for the adequate description of which no terms are discovered by the lexicographers of earth! And yet, the evidence drawn out in the cross-questioning shows that these inventions, which have been fulminated in court in the name of justice, were first rehearsed in the home of a minister of the gospel, who, in the name of the Christ, prayed for God's blessing on the fabrication in comparison with which cowardice is bravery, falsehood is truth, cruelty is kind, profanity model Sunday-school parlance, incendiarism a triviality and a pleasant pastime, thieving commendable enterprise, highway robbery majestic, and the inventions of fiendish ingenuity of but mild intensity! Aye, the bard, changing his numbers to fit the subject, would declare :—

' * * the foul wreath that murder wears,
Blood-nursed, and watered by a widow's tears,
Seems not so foul, so tainted, and so dread,
As waves the night-shade round the *slanderer's* head! '

"Earliest of the ' forty-niners ' from this region, Stephen Wilcutt in a few months found in the newly discovered El Dorado of our land gold enough to provide a fit home for the one he loved. And then came the news that he was murdered. He was a worthy man, and I have no doubt that he went to the rest awaiting the just. But let us suppose his departure to be in the present, and that the warder, meeting him at the outer gate, announces that before he can enter Elysium, he must do one of two noble acts, and that, because of his excellence, he may have his choice, and that choice is between forgiving the traducer of his wife's name and forgiving the one who took his earthly life! Both of the offenders are brought before him, when grasping the blood-red hand of the one who plunged the dagger to his bosom, he grants the slayer a full forgiveness, and, turning his back on the liar, walks through the wide-open gates to his reward with the blest!

"There I doubt not he waits and, looking from the serene heights, asks you to honor yourselves by granting an acquittal to those implicated in this most infamous indictment! One of them I have known for years and during that time have never heard the first lisp of obscenity from his lips and know that the whisper of unclean speech brings the blush to his cheek and arouses in him a healthy scorn for

the offender. And the other, since the going of her husband, has devoted herself to making garments for poor children and to ministrations
at the bedside of the sick ; and, in the course of her visitations she has
been again and again welcomed in the best homes, in that sacred moment when the mother looks for the first time on her offspring ! And
often with her gentle hand she has closed the eyes of the aged saint
to the last visions on earth before exaltation to the rare atmosphere
and beatific scenes of the hills of the Beyond !

"Mr. Foreman and Gentlemen—Here, in the name of your own
homes and in behalf of your fellow citizens, who ask you to stamp
this slander with disapproval, and thus put the contemptible business
of the Simpkins tongue at a discount; here, in the name of all you
hold dear; here, in this solemn hour and in this temple of justice,
whose walls have attested the oaths that hold you to righteous decision; here, I ask you, surrounded by these witnesses, and beheld I
I doubt not by those looking down from another world and speaking
to you in voices tremulous with tenderness and intense with earnestness—here and now, I ask you to grant a prompt acquittal to those
implicated in the monstrous findings brought for you to consider!
Then, with the approval of your conscience and of your God, go home
to receive, each of you, the sanction of the woman he loves, the admiration of the manly boys who are to copy the ways of their father, and
the love of those whose lives remind you of the lines of the bard,
voicing the sentiments of the Douglas as he beheld the fair Ellen :—

> ' Some feelings are to mortals given
> With less of earth in them than heaven ;
> And if there be a human tear
> From passion's dross refined and clear,
> A tear so limpid and so meek
> It would not stain an angel's cheek ;
> 'Tis that which pious fathers shed
> Upon a duteous daughter's head !'

"Acquit the accused, for they are as innocent of the wrongs with
which they are charged as is any one on this panel, any member of the
Wayfield bar, his honor Judge Robinson the magistrate on this occasion, or his kinsman the eminent Wayfield divine, who will thank me

for linking his name with those of my clients! As free are the accused of the befoulment named as are the waters of the mountain brook or the rays of the morning sun! Aye, gentlemen, they who could find aught of ill in the lives of those implicated in the indictment before you, would criticise the greetings of the saints on high and damn the behavior of Gabriel before the Throne!"

As Mr. Harrison closed, approval and delight was evident on the faces of all but those immediately interested in the prosecution, and there was a general feeling that he had won the jury to his view of the case, and that, whatever remarks Mr. Cheatham might make in presenting the other side, he could not counteract the effect of the burning words of the eloquent advocate for the defense. After a brief and perfunctory effort by the government's counsel, during which Mr. Harrison unconcernedly read a note handed him by an officer, in which note Mr. Barnes declared he would "hold the lawyer responsible for the offence to Simpkins," the judge arose to charge the jury, when there was a movement among the bystanders, and through the throng walked the well-known form of Elder Peters, who conferred a moment with Mr. Harrison, and the latter, arising, addressed the court :—

"If your honor please, I ask for a stay of proceedings, that newly discovered evidence may be introduced which is of vital importance to my clients."

Objections by Mr. Cheatham were promptly overruled, and the New Light preacher, called to the stand and sworn, testified that himself and daughter when returning

from a visit with a former parishioner, took shelter from
the great storm in the tenantless house formerly occupied
by Mr. Stedman's mother, and there remained until the
storm subsided.　He saw Stedman and Mrs. Wilcutt
come in and take seats in another room of the house,
where, facing the highway and facing from the witness,
they remained, and where, through a break in the parti-
tion they were by Mr Peters and his daughter seen, by
flashes of lightning that came at intervals of a moment,
until the storm was over; and there was none of the
wrong-doing charged against them.　The witness was
about to speak to them, when, the rain having ceased,
they walked away.　The witness then heard the cat-like
tread of some one in the chamber of the house, and, waiting a moment, he saw Simpkins leave as if in pursuit of
the two who had gone.　Business of importance called
Mr. Peters to churches in remote parts of the district the
next morning, and the first intimation he received of the
proceedings was the mention made of them in the Wayfield
News, a copy of which had reached him.　Then, thinking
the prosecution would include in their investigation the visit
of the accused to the Stedman house, he "followed the leadings of the Spirit," and, securing another minister to preside in his stead at a meeting of which he was moderator,
started at once for Wayfield and, as soon as arrived in
town, repaired to the court-house.

This testimony completed, Judge Robinson, arising,
said :—

"Mr. Foreman and Gentlemen—The court had meditated giving but brief instructions in a case where it was evident that justice was all on one side; and, with the unexpected light given by the truthful and intelligent witness who has just testified for the defense, and against whom the prosecution offer nothing in rebuttal, there remains but one thing for the court to do, and that is to instruct you, Mr. Foreman and gentlemen, to bring in, without leaving your seats, a verdict of not guilty on the indictment under consideration."

It was noticed that Mr. Harrison as he awaited the announcement of the verdict held a handkerchief, and that Officer Cushman carefully watched him and kept an eye also on Simpkins, who, strange to say, still tarried in the court-room. With the foreman's words "Not guilty," the silk dropped from Mr. Harrison's hand, and the officer, placing his hand on the shoulder of Simpkins, quietly said, "You are my prisoner, sir." The arrest was observed by Mr. Harrison, who arose, and, gathering up his papers, left the court-house. At his office he found Justice Edgerton, a Wayfield magistrate who had attended the trial in the higher court and before whom the papers for apprehending Simpkins were made returnable. Officer Cushman, who was crier of the court, asked the sheriff to appoint another deputy to act in his stead while he escorted his man into the presence of Edgerton. Mr. Harrison said in presenting the case :—

"If your Honor please : Counsel desired that the case which, without—noticeably without—the customary hearing before a magistrate, was brought in the higher court, against his clients, should be tried on its own merits; and he did not make use of a fact which he might have taken to hinder the prosecution, a fact that would have damaged

the reputation of their principal witness. By the revelation that might
have been made he would have appeared not only the slanderer which
his previous reputation warranted counsel in calling him, but guilty
of the very crime which he had the audacity to charge upon those
now deservedly declared by a jury of their peers to be innocent! And
now, may it please your Honor, I propose to prove that the scoundrel
whom in that trial I denounced as a liar is as foul as he is false !   On
a warrant given by Esquire Albert Belmont, whose care in issuing
complaints is deservedly proverbial, the fellow figuring as chief mover
in the prosecution now happily terminated has just been arrested by
an officer who, with other truthful witnesses, will substantiate the
charges made in the precept accusing him of a crime which the sneak-
ing, trembling Simpkins supposed known only to him and his *parti-
ceps criminis*! The warrant meditates bringing the accused before a
magistrate of the court below, by whom, if he is remanded to await
the action of the grand jury, his case will then be in order for trial in
the higher court. But, in the alternative which I shall propose for the
consideration of the judge presiding in the upper court, he will find an
easier solution of the problem before him, an alternative which I advise him to accept, for the proof is so conclusive that a trial in that
court can but result in a verdict of guilty and the full sentence allowed
by law. If the defendant consents now to a plea of guilty in that
court, when he comes up there for sentence, I shall ask that the judge,
in the discretion allowed him, impose but a light sentence, and thus,
in his leniency, show mercy on him who showed no mercy !

"In contrast to the unparalleled proceedings instigated by Simpkins, I shall ask your Honor to continue the case which is brought
against him and hear it a week later, asking this postponement that
the prisoner may have ample time to secure counsel to represent him
at the trial."

Required by Justice Edgerton to furnish bail in the
sum of five hundred dollars with ample sureties for his
re-appearance at the hearing a week later, Simpkins tarried with the justice while an acquaintance of the former

went to importune Deacon Lemuel Barnes to become
bondsman with Deacon David Grout, who had been visiting Barnes and had accompanied him to the trial. But,
"foreordained and elected unto heaven" though they
were, they had none of the heavenly quality of pity, and
Sam Simpkins, now that he was in trouble and circum-
stanced so that Deacon "Lem" could not use him as a
cat's paw, was refused the boon he asked and was ordered
to be "committed in default."

Mr. Harrison, who had occasion to revisit the court-
house, came in just as Dr. Johnson and Mr. Stedman,
who, on the announcement of the verdict had left the
place of trial, returned from a drive to the house of Mrs.
Wilcutt. Stedman dropping into the first chair he found,
Dr. Johnson approached Mr. Harrison and whispered a
few words, when the lawyer, turning pale, approached the
bench, and, as Judge Robinson leaned forward, whispered:—

"Mrs. Wilcutt, the lovely woman who was one of the
victims of this most cruel slander, and whose absence
from the excitements of the trial was so grudgingly allowed by the prosecution on the physician's certificate
that her prostration under the accusation was such that it
would be impossible for her to retain her reason and be
in the court-room—this excellent one has gone where the
wicked cease from troubling. She lived until Dr. Johnson and her friend arrived with the news of the findings
of the jury. And, with a smile at the thought that the

stigma was removed from her name, she extended her hand to Mr. Stedman and breathed her last—murdered by the Simpkins tongue!"

The news of the fatal effect of the venomous falsehood was soon known to all in the court-room and to a throng gathered at the door of Harrison's office, and who, it was evident, would be likely to handle Simpkins roughly did they get hold of him. Learning the situation, Officer Cushman, when Mr. Stedman came in with his counsel, asked the former to pacificate his would-be friends who thought by personal violence to the slanderer to avenge the wrong done his victim. And through the kindness of Thomas Stedman, whom he had slandered, Samuel Simpkins in charge of an officer walked undisturbed to the imprisonment which was but a part of that which he merited for crime like that he had industriously and unsuccessfully tried to fasten upon the one on whom he now had to depend for his safety!

There was another after-piece to the drama of the Stedman trial. When, the day following the commitment of Simpkins to jail, it became known to the prisoners that he was there, the turnkey discovered evidence of dissatisfaction at something on the faces of even the most tractable and obedient of the inmates, not excepting Jacob Sanders, "Big Jake" as he was called, who, in serving his sentence of a year for an encounter with a "Scrabble Hollow" fellow, had made the exceptionally good record that entitled him to the greatest reduction of time allowed

by law and who, with this "cut-down," had but a month
more to remain. That evening, at the half-hour of "hall
liberty" granted the prisoners between supper and "lock-
up time," they met, "resolved," and sent "Big Jake," as
the one most in favor with the prison authorities, to make
known to them the meaning of the meeting. Appearing
before Sheriff Walbridge the prison-keeper, who knew
that Mrs. Wilcutt's missionary work had included kindness to the children of the poor, and that Jake's little
ones had been the recipients of the benefactions of this
Dorcas, the rough man told the officer of what the good
woman had done, and wiping away the tears of tenderness
that the thought of her deeds had caused, thus concluded
his speech :—

"We's ben fightin', stealin', an' breakin' inter housen, an' it's all
right ter punish us; but it's tew bad fer us ter hev ter 'sosherate with
sech a feller ez would sen' out his pizen tork erbout sech er angil ez
Mis' Wilcutt thet Simpkins hez murdered by his cussed lies. An' we
wish thet you'd hev him eat in his cell an' not march with us to git
rations."

"Jake, it's all right," said Mr. Walbridge, "I know
you are honest; and you can go back and tell the men that
the turnkey will send Simpkins his rations at his cell.
But you needn't tell them that I am going to reward you
for your good behavior while in prison. It's but a month
more you have to serve, and during that time you may
spend your forenoons in the hall, and in the afternoons you
will be given work in the grounds where you can breathe

the air of the out-door world and hear the birds and find something to divert your mind from prison life. Do you know Elder Peters?"

"Yis,—" and the warm tears of gratitude and joy that coursed down the rough features completed the utterance.

"Well, he's interceded with the commissioners, and conferred with Mr. Harrison who was prosecuting attorney when you was convicted, and they ar.d he consented to the request of Mr. Peters, and the result is instruction to me to give you the reward of which I have told you, and it includes also, at my request, your assignment to quarters in a large room in another part of the prison building, where you will have a better bed and more room. The law compels me to lock you in and keep the key, but the place will be far better than a cell."

"Mr. Walbridge, the likes o' me hain't fit ter hev sech blessin's, but—" and sobbing for joy, the poor man dropped kneeling on the floor at the sheriff's feet, and laying his hands on the officer's knees, he looked up and said :—

"Elder Peters hez been the makin' o' me. 'Twas he that curridged me when I felt as if the devil had me sure, an' then I tried to be good ; and now I hev all this privilege an' I kin try ter be a man, when I git out o' here."

"All right, Jake," said Sheriff Walbridge. But he did not tell the man what Jake found out when, on being dismissed two days before the completion of his time, he was told to call at the store of Payson Sherwood & Son. There he found work as a porter awaiting him, with a

place to sleep given him in the building, and with the
privilege of three hours a day to himself, which he used
in doing odd jobs at the office of Mr. Harrison and about
his grounds. Mr. Peters kept up his interest in the man,
and was rewarded by the upright life that Sanders lived.
The fact that Elder Peters was interested in him induced
others to copy the minister's friendliness. And Jake
Sanders won many friends at Wayfield, and the children,
seeing the respect that was shown their father, began to
lead good lives. His wife who had not taken avail of his
imprisonment, the fact of which would have been sufficient grounds for a divorce, accepted him after his release;
and the pleasant domestic life of Jake Sanders was remarked by all who knew him.

Eloquent in their fitness were the words spoken by
Elder Peters to the company of sincere mourners at the
funeral of the good and beautiful Mrs. Wilcutt. And loving hands made her grave on a sunny slope near the
grasses growing above the remains of the son of her
friends the Taylors, and in a territory which was soon
after dedicated as a "God's Acre," and given the name of
"Hill-side Rest," and on the arched entrance to which
were inscribed the fitting words, "Until the day break."
The floral offerings adorning the casket that enclosed
her form were bestowed by Agnes Smith and others of
the New Light young people who "sorrowed that they
should see her face no more;" and the rose they planted

by the resting place of this Dorcas of Dayville bloomed
on through all the joyous Junes to remind that her spirit,
freed from the ills of the earthly life and reunited forever
with her consort, inhaled the fragrance and rejoiced in
the beauty of the flowers of the eternal hills !

Events of such interest as the trial and triumphant vin-
dication of Mr. Stedman and his friend, the death of one
of the victims and the deserved disgrace of the instigator
of the prosecution, were thought by the managers of the
News to be of sufficient interest to warrant issuing, the
day before the regular paper, an "extra" giving the account of the proceedings, and a large edition was sold in
two hours after it had been printed, while the enlarged
issue on the regular day of publication fell far short of
the demand.

When Rev. Dr. Robinson saw fit to make allusion in a
sermon to an event of popular interest, his remarks were
in the best of taste and fully comporting with the dignity
appropriate to pulpit ministrations ; and if denuncia-
tions of wrong-doing were in order, they were made in
that masterly way that commanded respect.   And when,
the Sunday following the great trial, the Wayfield divine
closed a discourse on the sin of speaking evil, there was
the stillness of death as, in completing his picture of a
slanderer, he declared, " ' He shall be driven from light
into darkness, and chased out of the world ! ' "   And it is

safe to say that the portrait arising to the mind's eye of every one, was that of Samuel Simpkins !

Further "improvement" of the case which had been the subject of his sermon, the minister made in the following letter, which, like all his acts, was its own warrant and carried its own explanation :—

" *To the Editor of the Wayfield News :—*

On perusing the full and fair account of the trial and deserved acquittal of Mr. Stedman and the lady whose name was associated with his, which last week appeared in your journal, and the fitting editorial comment made on 'the sin and mischief of slander,' I sought, but did not find, extra copies of the paper to send as 'tracts' to a neighboring parish where there are those who forget the commandment that forbids bearing false witness against one's neighbor. Returning from the fruitless search I thought to ask you to reprint as much as your crowded space would allow of account and comment, and let me ask you not to omit the truthful and tender allusions made by Mr. Harrison to the lovely Agnes Stuart ; for I shall want to send to her friends in Scotland evidence from so good authority that she was held in high esteem by the best people of this region, that here, where she whose life was the efflorescence and fragrance of helpfulness, goodness and joy, suffered death by the sting of a Simpkins slander, her name is still revered and loved, as is that of her friend Ralph Jameson, whose association with her was indeed beautiful and who was another victim of the venom of the serpent Simpkins. Asking you to grant this favor, and thanking you for the attention you have already given this subject, and for what you have thus done towards making slander seem the contemptible thing that it really is, I am,

Very truly yours,

R. H. ROBINSON."

Although Lemuel Barnes and his brother deacon from Hardland at first refused to become sureties for Simpkins, they afterwards concluded, for some reason, " to go his

bail ; " and when at the hearing before the magistrate the
fellow was required to furnish bonds in five hundred dollars, to await the action of the grand jury at the next
criminal term, Barnes and Grout readily became his sureties. Bill Jones, who, having completed his rounds as
market gardener, happened in at the office of Mr. Harrison, remarked to an acquaintance :—

"I'll venter a V thet some one's ben tellin' Simpkins
erbaout ole Barnes's dewin's consarnin' the Atherton venshuns, ef Simpkins didn't know on't afore. An' Deekin
Lem and Deekin Grout faound aout erbaout ther tellin',
an' kinder thort thet Simpkins would tell erbaout the
crookedness ef they didn't git him aout uv jail."

Jones, who had entrusted to Mike Tobin the over-
sight of the hands demanded by his growing business,
and who continued the familiarity of comradeship which
obtained between the two when they were fellow farm
laborers at Barnes's, confided to him, on returning home,
the opinion which he had given the attorney. And to his
foreman, three months later, he remarked, when Simpkins
chanced to be the subject of conversation, as gardener
and overseer were "slicking up things" about the grounds
of the Jones establishment:—

"I say, Mike Tobin, s'posin' the feller sh'd run erway
an' ole Barnes hev ter pay the bail money uv five hunnud
dollars ! Wouldn't that air be a good joke on the ole man !"

"It would, thin, Bill Joanes, an' shure. An' 'pon me
sowl, an' 'twould be sarvin' him right ; an', begorry, Bill

Joanes, if 'twouldn't, thin; for, shure, he got his money by stalin' the Atherton vinshuns!"

On coming back from Wayfield five days later, Jones thus exclaimed as he threw down the lines to his foreman, who appeared to unharness the gardener's horse :—

"I say, Mike, that air Simpkins hez ben an' done it—'drawd his sled' in the night, an' gone 'hook an' line, bob and sinker,' clean erway daown inter Conneckticut!"

"Just loike the sarpint, thin, for shure the snake that bites will run, thin! An', say, owld Barruns will hev ter pay the—what do yez call it?—the bail money."

"Sure as preachin', Mike Tobin; fer Square Harrison'll not let the grass grow under his feet afore he makes ole Barnes come daown with 'the ready.' It's a curis state uv things, though; fer, yer see, it b'longs ter ole Cheatham ter make a move fer the bail money ter be 'forked over,' naow thet Simpkins hez scud orf, the same ez 'twould a-b'long'd ter him ter prosecute Simpkins, ef he'd a-ben on han' fer trial. An' Cheatham'll not want ter budge er inch ter put Simpkins threw. But Square Harrison'll 'make it hot' fer him ef he don't hev the guvner bled ter wunst, ter the tune uv five hunnud dollars fer the good uv the state!"

On his return the next day from Wayfield, Jones thus saluted Tobin :—

"I hearn to-day thet Simpkins an' Hetty Simpkins, she 't wuz, went orf tergether. An', yer see thet ole Barnes, afore he'd go bail fer Simpkins, had Hetty mortgidge ter

him the place thet Atherton left her, Atherton what wuz
as much better'n Hetty Simpkins thet wuz tied ter him ez
a rose is better'n mud, or a robin better'n a hornet. This
wuz dun kinder 'on the sly,' an' Simpkins he, somehow er
other, got all his b'longin's inter money an' made Hetty
good in part fer what she'd mortgidged ter Barnes; an'
they 'vamoosed the ranch' in the night, as I said afore.
An' naow comes the nub on't, all! An' Hetty Simpkins
thet wuz sech a torment ter Atherton an' scoldid erbaout
him over his dead body hez ben killed in 'most jes' the
same way thet he wuz! An' I b'lieve there's a proverden-
tial han' in it all, so's ter teach folks better'n ter be cruel!"

"'Pon me sowl, Bill Joanes, ef Moike Tobin ever hayerd
the loikes uv it afore, an' shure, Bill Joanes, thin, begorry,
at all at all! But its thrue fer yez, Bill Joanes. An' 'pon
me sowl ther'll be nary a one ter care ef this owld taarmint
is gone!"

"Your right, Mike Tobin. An', as luck would have it,
the scold was thrown daown er bank inter a stream what
the storm had riz so's 't carried her daown inter the Conneckticut which wuz a-ragin' like ole Jurdan! An' Hetty
Simpkins, she thet wuz, wuz flooded daown ter Long
Islan' Saoun'!"

"An' fwhat wuz the cause uv the accidint, Bill Joanes,
I dunno? Did yez mane there wuz a runaway loike the
one whin Atherton an' Square Willums wuz killed?"

"Well, yer see, erbaout four o'clock in the arternoon, ez
the naburz obsarved what teld the story ter Mr. Dorson

whut wuz a-visitin' 'mong the folks where he used ter
peddle, Simpkins an' Het wuz a-drivin' erlong an' a piece
o' paper thet some one hed throwed aout wuz whirled up by
a gust o' wind, in front uv their hoss, an' th' ole plug, ez
some ole plugs will thet look ez ef they couldn't dror a
shadder, jes' frisked up an' run, spite uv all Sam could do,
an' Het a-screamin' like house-o'-fire, an' the hoss struck
the waggin agin a post uv the railin' nigh ter a bridge, an'
there wuz a capsize, Het a-gwine inter the drink ! But the
pizen thing erbaout it all is thet Simpkins wuz only
stunned, an' half er aour arterwurds wuz fetched to, by
the naburz what picked him up. But Mike Tobin, yer
can jes' bet thet he'll never come back ter these diggin's
agin."

Officer Cushman took from an inner pocket, as he
entered his house on a pleasant street of Wayfield, a writ
of *scire facias* directed "to the sheriffs of our several coun-
ties and their deputies, greeting," and running :—

"Whereas Samuel Simpkins of Wayfield, Lemuel Barnes of Dayville and David Grout of Hardland personally appeared before the
court of common pleas and acknowledged themselves to be indebted
to the commonwealth in the sum of five hundred dollars ; * * *
and whereas the said Simpkins, Barnes and Grout, although solemnly
called to come into court, did not appear, * * * we therefore
* * * command you that you make known to the said Simpkins,
Barnes and Grout," * * *

Opening, scanning and again folding the document and
noting on the back the words, " By virtue of the within

precept I have this day notified," * * * the officer affixed, in a clear hand, the signature of "Theodore Cushman, Deputy Sheriff." Then, placing the paper in his desk, he said, as he seated himself near a little woman who was busied with sewing, the while with a foot she gently rocked a cradle in which was a boy baby that seemed a picture of his sire :—

"Ethel, that Barnes will have to settle for the Simpkins bail, now that the fellow has gone. But it will only be a 'drop in the bucket' to what he has made from the Atherton inventions which he stole. And I think he has ample security in the Atherton place mortgaged to him by Simpkins's sister."

"And it seems too bad that the property left by Mr. Atherton should not go to the boy whom it would do so much good in defraying, in part, the expenses of an education. How hard it is that Barnes who stole the inventions of Mr. Atherton's brain should take also the little sum of the inventor's savings and leave his orphan boy penniless! But, mark my word, Theodore,"—and the earnest woman laid a hand tenderly on the arm of her husband—"mark my word, there'll something come, I know not how, nor when, nor where, but there'll something come to remind the selfish and grasping man of his injustice and fraud! Such is my impression ; and I believe in impressions, and who would not believe in them, who has seen that Elder Peters, in following the 'leadings of the spirit,' as he calls it, comes into the right place at the right time !"

"When Charlie Newton of Hardland, as we sat in court not long after Mr. Peters brought the boy Atherton from Hardland, told me the story of the timely rescue of the lad from the keeping of Grout who was inflicting a most inhuman scourging, one more blow of which, as Doctor Johnson declared when he reached the sufferer, would have crushed out his reason forever, I said to myself, 'There must be something in the elder's idea of heeding the voice within.' By the way, Ethel, at the Stedman trial Barnes wrote a note to Mr. Harrison on the completion of the lawyer's argument for his clients and which missive, as Mr. Harrison afterward informed me, called him to account for his arraignment of Simpkins. I had noticed at the time that he placed the letter carefully in his pocket, and something then seemed to say to me 'That specimen of Barnes's handwriting may be used as evidence against him some time.'"

Lemuel Barnes, deacon of the Dayville church of Christ, chairman of the standing committee, and, as ever, "foreordained and elected unto eternal salvation," was apprized by the jailer that the slanderer had learned of his dark secret concerning the inventions and was alive to the fact that Simpkins, though in prison, had him at his mercy. And though, conscious of his consequence as a member of the aristocracy of theological correctness and as an heir, by predestination, to the bliss of heaven, he nevertheless thought it wise to grant Simpkins the favor of his name as surety to the government on the bail-bond of the man. Others too, had whispered hints indicating that they surmised there was "a cat under the meal," and when it became known that Simpkins had absconded Barnes concluded to "pay up" at once. And the very day that the officer called on him he deposited the required sum with the clerk of courts. Informing his brother deacon at Hardland of the juncture of affairs, he received a call from that worthy the next day, when the latter gave Barnes half of the money forfeited by the escapade of Simpkins.

As Grout returned home he was met by Tim Edgerley, who thus saluted him :—

"Twuz tew bad tew hev tew pay fer that air Simpkins runnin' orf, ez I s'pose ye did; an' ole Barnes orter hev paid the hull bizness, fer he's well on't, specially sence he's had those venshuns o' Atherton's; an' that air Atherton place thet wuz mortgidged tew him'll more'n pay the bill thet he had tew 'fork over.' An,' Dave Grout, I pity ye, yis I dew ! But Dave Grout, yer ortn't ter hev gone in with Barnes erbaout those venshuns. Fer Barnes, who's got the best on ye this time, 'll dew it agin. The feller whut steals from one an' gits some one else tew help him dew it, will steal from the feller whut helps him as well as from 'tother ! "

And is it asked how was young Atherton affected by the death of his mother ? by the death of the woman who was the maternal parent of his physical self? What could he think who had not received from her the first evidence of motherly love? What could he think who had starved for a mother's love, and who for the first expression of it would have made quick return from the abundance of his own royal nature? Would he mourn, who, unloved by the mother of his physical being, found, at last, the wants of his starved nature satisfied by the love of two noble women who had taken him to the home of their hearts? Often had he mourned that he had no mother. Often had he mourned that his mother was not his mother. Would he mourn when she died who was not his mother? He was indeed shocked that she was so rudely torn from life, and had her form been recovered his regard for the name of mother would have found expression in asking that a decent interment be given the remains of the one who bore that name, albeit she was no mother! Even the very power to endure the shock of her sudden and untimely taking off came from his consciousness that others loved him. And from that love came the courage to try to recover from the crushing he had experienced from a tyrannical will and to try and bear the sorrow of the loss of him who was not only father of his physical being but the father of his soul.

CHAPTER III.

WHATEVER the faults of some holding that office, there were good deacons as well as bad ones; and what a deacon should be was shown in the sterling worth and beautiful life of Payson Sherwood of the Wayfield church of the standing order. The genuineness of his piety no one could doubt, and it won him the respect of all, the worldly as well as the religious.

Among those outside "the fold" who respected him was Mr. Harrison, the infidel, who cherished for him not only respect, but warm friendship—a friendship that grew with every passing year. And the two had mutual likings for Reverend Doctor Robinson, whose sermons Deacon Sherwood seldom missed hearing and from whose ministrations Mr. Harrison was always absent. The kindness of Deacon Sherwood to the poor was known to everybody, although it accorded, in the bestowment, with the Scriptural injunction, "Let not thy left hand know what thy right doeth." He loved children, and the Sunday school where they learned the story of the Christ had charms for him. By his associate workers crowded into the office of Superintendent, he filled the place with efficiency for a dozen years, until, on his positive refusal to serve longer, they

chose, in his stead, his son Payson Sherwood, Jr., who
served five years and went back to teaching a class. This
gentleman resembled his father and his mother, and both
parents rejoiced to see repeated in him the traits they
loved in each other. And these admirable qualities they
found again repeated in the grandson, little John Sherwood,
whose mother thought more of her husband's parents than
of her own, and was rewarded with parental affection that
could not have been greater had its object been the offspring of the life of those who bestowed that love.

Duly prizing the fact of a liberal education, and conscious that those who knew him best thought him well
worthy the college parchment he possessed, Deacon Sherwood was not vain of their opinion, and modest and in-
frequent were his references to his years at Yale. While

> " His library, though large, was read
> Till half its contents decked his head,"

he seldom mentioned the fact that he had perused more
books than any other man in Wayfield, Doctor Robinson
not excepted. And of this fact he learned only when
driven by the divine, in a good-natured banter of minister
and deacon, to compare notes as to the tomes each had
conned. Deacon Sherwood was a temperance man on
conviction and not because he had a cold temperament
and lacked the generous impulses which might prompt him
to bestow wines in his hospitality. He advocated the temperance cause and did it fearlessly, not to make himself
prominent but for the good he hoped to accomplish. And

though earnest in his advocacy of the cause, he did not
seek to make himself personally obnoxious to the opponents of temperance. His convictions on the subject
were genuine and he had the courage of his convictions.
That genuineness and fearlessness won him the respect
of the opponents of the cause. And they knowing the
popular regard for the generous, sincere and public-spirited
man, concluded, whenever he was in nomination for office,
to make that their "off year" and to do little more than
"go through the motions" of opposing his candidacy. So
it was that, in 1857, when nominated for the Legislature,
he received a majority of three to one for the man who
consented to be the forlorn hope of the other side. Mr.
Harrison, who was candidate for the Senate, received a
peculiarly flattering indorsement at the polls, and he at
once took high rank as legislator. Although it had
been for a long time the rule not to award the chairmanship of any committee to a new member though he might
be fully fitted for the place, the managers of the dominant
party thought it well to make an exception in the case of
Mr. Harrison, and he was given the chairmanship of the
judiciary. The same exception was made in favor of his
friend and townsman in the House, where the head of the
committee on banks and banking was Payson Sherwood of
Wayfield; and Mr. Stedman, whose friends, to express
their esteem for the man and to give an emphatic rebuke
to those who had instigated the prosecution from which he
had so triumphantly come, secured his re-election to the

House by a majority far exceeding the one he received at his election, was awarded the chairmanship of the committee on highways and bridges.

It was natural that the three men, who had tastes in common, should, in their experience at the Legislature, increase their mutual liking. They occupied adjacent lodgings in the same hotel and at evening the trio, in the room of one of their number, compared notes in reference to the besiegings they had endured from the lobbyists, and discussed measures which were in order for the day following. The week's work at the capitol over, they were sure to take passage by the next train of the recently completed Wayfield railroad to the town that named the same. Thence, bidding his friends good-bye, Mr. Stedman drove rapidly to his home with the Smiths of Dayville, where, after scanning, at his offce, the important letters of the patrons of his factory enterprise, which his clerk had left for his inspection, he received calls from those who had business with him as legislator. And one of these, of an evening midway in the term, was his minister and friend, Elder Peters, who still had rooms at the Smith homestead. After a brief conference he called in Mr. Smith; and the result of the interview developed when, a fortnight later, "an act to incorporate Daniel Smith, Thomas Stedman, Samuel Taylor, Albert Belmont, and Luke Johnson, their successors and associates, as the Dayville Library Association," was introduced by Mr. Sherwood in the House and passed without debate, as it was in the Senate, where the measure was presented by Mr. Harrison. Another bill advocated by the same gentlemen incorporated the "Hillside Cemetery Association," with the same names and others on the list of corporators.

Naturally Deacon Sherwood was friend and confidant of his minister; and naturally the divine, who had received three obtrusive and censorious letters from the Dayville centre minister, handed the third missive to Mr. Sherwood as the latter called on his minister, of an afternoon, and said :—

"Friend Sherwood, what shall I do with that Brother Barber of mine? Look. at this letter of his and tell me what you think of it?"

"If so you wish, Doctor, I'll try to answer him."

"Capital!—and I'll thank you to take the task off my hands."

And the twinkle of wit in Sherwood's eyes heightened to indignation as he walked to the counting-room of the store where "Payson Sherwood & Son" carried on the mercantile business founded by John Sherwood. There, an hour later, the deacon handed his son the following letter, which the latter read with evident delight, and handed back to his father, as Jake Sanders, the porter, came in for the letters of the day to post :—

"REVEREND SIR :—

The great demands on him for pastoral work, to say nothing of the study he holds himself bound to give to the preparation for his pulpit efforts, leave Reverend Doctor Robinson little time for correspondence and he has accepted my offer to reply to the letter which you recently sent, calling him to account for alleged decadence from old-time standards of orthodox theology. You question him for preaching sermons which show that he thinks that 'God so loved the world that He gave His only begotten Son, that whosoever believeth in Him should not perish but have everlasting life!' You find fault with discourses that breathe the spirit of that culminating harmony of the grand song of the seer of Patmos, and proclaim that 'Whosoever will' may be saved through the provisions of the gospel of the Christ! You criticise that which is the crowning glory of His gospel, that to which point promises and prophecies that give the older Scriptures their significance, that which was the theme of the heavenly host o'er Bethlehem's plains, that whose full meaning is beyond the possibilities of the human ken in a lifetime to discern, and that which shall come to its full unfolding only somewhere in the happy eternities!

Allow me to say, sir, that I am of the opinion that this kind of preaching is acceptable to a large proportion of the hearers of the speaker whose ideas have so excited your apprehension, and that should your criticisms of their minister be made known to them, the strictures would greatly lessen whatever of respect they may entertain for the one who has assumed the role of censor. You find fault with Doctor Robinson for his 'leaning toward' the doctrines of the New Lights, recognizing their Elder Peters as a minister and associating with him. To these charges the one you criticise would be proud to 'plead guilty;' and because of his liking for the followers of Wesley, his own people of the standing order like the Wayfield divine. Right cordially do they appreciate the sermons which Mr. Peters gives them from the pulpit of Doctor Robinson, discourses which I doubt not will be long remembered for the truths they contain and the fervor of eloquence with which they are delivered. I presume that the pastor of the Wayfield church had no thought of being specially wise in asking Elder Peters to his pulpit and in his other acts of Christian courtesy, only as all such acts are wise, but he could not have done anything more likely to build up his own church and denomination than he has done in his cordial and unmistakable recognition of the New Lights.

You also mention as evidence of Doctor Robinson's divergence from the regulation way of thinking, his 'associating with an infidel lawyer.' referring, I presume, to his well known friendship for that able attorney and excellent gentleman, Esquire Andrew M. Harrison, whose interest in the temperance cause and in the cause of education certainly entitle him to the respect of the people, and whose learning and culture make him a most companionable man. If such qualities are not in themselves full warrant for the minister to associate with Mr. Harrison, there is the additional fact to be considered that prominent among the ladies of the church, and necessarily called to coöperate with him in parish work, is Mrs. Harrison. And I cannot think the one I am addressing so dull as not to see that it would be hardly wise for a minister to refuse to associate with a gentleman whose wife he was frequently called to meet.

And, now, sir, permit me to say in closing that further evidence that Doctor Robinson is right in his course may be found in the growth of his church in all that gives a church significance and renders it helpful in the work of elevating humanity. And permit me also to say that if you think there will be many to join in your censure of Rowland Hill Robinson, for his acts or his theological opinions, so thinks not

PAYSON SHERWOOD."

Timothy Edgerley remained at the Sumner farm at Hardland, until late in 1857, and the following letter showing his whereabouts two years later, reveals a marked improvement in his language, tells us how the betterment came about, gives full evidence that his love for the woman of his choice has not diminished, and tells what she is doing and has done, and what high enjoyments are his:

"NEW YORK, October 19, 1859.

MY OWN DEAR JENNIE:—

Most heartily do I thank you for the letter you last sent me, as I do for all the many pleasant epistles which your regard for me has prompted. They breathe the spirit of true devotion, show an unwavering loyalty of heart and inspire me to a full reciprocation of the sentiments they manifest. Yes, my own, I am yours, and yours not only because I wish to be yours, but because your love leads me to be yours. It is all with you, all as you make it. So, it seems to me, the case is with every true woman—she generally, though not invariably, receives about that which she invites—awakens her lover to be, inspires him to be, about the man she wants him to be. But my own, you understand better than do I this concerning which I am philosophizing.

Dearest, I now wish to thank you for the discipline which you instituted for me, looking towards the improvement of my speech, discipline which, at the time, seemed very severe, indeed so severe that had I not loved you I could not have submitted to it, however much I might have needed the improvement then meditated, and, I trust, now realized. Always shall I remember with pleasure the studying I did, mornings and evenings, when working for Mr. Smith at Dayville, when you were teaching the village school. The 'language lessons' which, at your asking, Mrs. Smith prescribed for me to learn, at first seemed very difficult to master, but, the fact that you loved me nerved me to undertake the work, and by dint of much application I succeeded at last. You wished me to practice what I had learned and insisted on a promise, which at last I gave, and up to which I then tried, and still try, to act, a promise that I would do my best to speak correctly even in making the most inconsequential remark in conversation on ordinary matters. Some of the books which you suggested for perusal and which then I read, I have since re-read and have found them not only entertaining in story and in style, but helpful to me in the endeavor to converse with correctness. Irving's works were indeed charming and I took delight in reading Addison's writings, and for English, commend me to King James's translation of the psalms of David, the prayer at the dedication of the temple at Jerusalem, the Sermon on the Mount, and Peter's sermon at the Pentecost, with its fiery philippic of denunciation of the murderers of Christ, whom he brought face to face with 'the teeth and forehead of their faults.' And thus, I quote the great Shakespeare, some of the passages of the best of whose plays I have read with great benefit, while I have also found interest in, and help from, perusing the tales of 'good old Father Chaucer.'

Dearest, I am glad that you have such fine companionship as is

yours at the home of the Harrisons, where, as your letters reveal, you
have not a little time with that accomplished lady, Mrs. Harrison, who
is so kind as to introduce you into the best society of the town, as her
friend.   And I am glad you are to remain with her another year.

Cousin Darling is doing well in mercantile business, here in New
York, and has just been admitted a partner in the firm that has em-
ployed him.   Remember me kindly to his Mary when you write to
her, and inform me of their day as soon as you ascertain the date, for
Lew will want me to attend.   My position as superintendent of out-
door work, in connection with a large manufacturing establishment,
is on the whole pleasant; and, while the duties of the place keep me
busy during the day, my evenings and Sundays give me time for not
a little reading.   Just at present I am perusing the Titcomb letters,
which I find full of advice, that is not only wholesome, as advice to
the young often is, but relishable, as most advice to the young is not,
and advice that is well and even entertainingly told.   Occasionally I
attend a lecture, and the military company of fine young men, to
which I belong, and in which I have been chosen lieutenant, meets
every week for exercise in manual and maneuver.   So days and evenings are well filled, my health is fairly good, and asking you to pray
that I be grateful for the blessings that are mine, that I try first,
to be worthy of them and then to improve them, I am, dearest,

Always yours,
TIMOTHY EDGERLEY."

Associating with one who is spiritually minded awakens the soul of one of less spiritual endowment to the
significance and the importance of spiritual things.   And
when, through the planning of her lover, Jennie Davis
"from the Ammynoosick regin ov Noo Hampshear," as
ran Edgerley's letter anent the matter, came to teach the
higher grade of the Dayville school, and boarded with
Mrs. Smith, the young woman soon gave evidence of the
possibility of a great deal of spiritual life, and began a

soul growth, which, in its later developments, was surprising even to the spiritual woman with whom she had her home. The influence of Mrs. Smith, who, from the first, invited the younger woman to a nearness of companionship, was a great stimulus to this growth, which had still other help in the work of teaching that brought the teacher into closer relations with the young, especially with Agnes Smith, whose discerning mind, sweet temper, and unselfishness of heart and life, influenced all her mates for good and inspired her teacher. With this girl as leader among the children, and with Miss Davis for instructor, the Dayville school became source and centre of the most joyous young life of all the region— most joyous, unless it was that of the same children on Sundays in the Dayville Bible school of the New Lights. Therein Mrs. Smith and many of the women of her acquaintance, unaided by lesson papers, blackboards, globes, and other Sunday school traps and machinery of the moderns, taught the Word to the young minds committed to their care, gently but effectually instilled gospel truth into their hearts, and charmed them with the story of Jesus. And in this scene of life and joy, Jennie Davis found still another stimulus to her growth of soul.

It was natural that Mrs. Smith should take an interest in the welfare of her friend's lover, especially as he was one of those who had befriended the boy for whom she had a great love, and for whose well-being she had the solicitude of a mother. She saw that Edgerley, who had

real manliness, a gentle nature and much native ability,
lacked elegance of speech, and that such a deficiency
might keep him from the society of those to whose companionship he would by his excellent qualities be entitled
and towards which, by the exhibition of those, qualities, he
would be led. Thus, too, thought Jennie Davis, the awakening of whose spiritual nature had, of course, increased her
love for the man she prized, and had, also, quickened her
vision to see not only his many excellences but his few
defects. And when Mrs. Smith, to whom impressions had
the authority of divine commands, and who had learned
that it was well to heed them, suggested to her friend that
it was important for Edgerley to improve in speech and
eminently fit that she should speak of the matter to him,
the idea was received favorably by Miss Davis. When
the subject was mentioned to Edgerley, though the great-
ness of the undertaking seemed at first to overpower him,
and he shrunk from the work which it would involve,
he soon promised his hearty coöperation. And when, to
any one, Timothy Edgerley gave his word that he would do
anything, that word was kept. How binding, then, must he
have regarded his promise to Jennie Davis to "try to learn
to talk right!" And to this she responded, as a smile
brightened her face :—

"Dearest, you will be sure to succeed; for Timothy
Edgerley never undertakes anything which he does not
carry to completion. You will have my heartiest interest
all the time, and if you think I can be of any help to you

in your studies, be free to ask me, and you can be sure
that if I am teacher of Timothy Edgerley, I shall not be
his dictator but rather a learner by his side, a companion
of his journey up the hill which he is to climb!"

What would Edgerley say but that which he did say, as,
bending, he kissed her lips and tenderly with his giant
hand caressed her auburn locks: "Yes, Jennie, and I
shall owe you much for the success you hope I am to
win. Tell me what I am to do; for I want to begin the
work at once."

"And you have already taken one step in the journey."

"Well, I always talk best when there's something large
to talk about, as there is likely to be when you are present."

"Thank you, my own."

And the two, as if moved by a common impulse, knelt,
and the prayer of Jennie Davis was the petition of each :—
"O Father in heaven, accept our thanks for all the
blessings that come from Thy bountiful hand. Grant us
each the grace we need for the work that is now before
us, grace for all the work of life, grace to bravely meet and
go through the emergency of life's termination and fitness
for the reward of the blest, beyond!" And Edgerley's letter has told us what answer was vouchsafed the peti-
tioners, who went to work to answer their own prayers.

In the summer of 1859 the Dayville Library Association
erected a building of neat architectural design, on Main
Street nearly opposite the residence of the Smiths.

The October days of that year have come and the morning appointed for the opening of the library dawns bright with glorious sunshine, in which the maples glow with their wealth of crimson and gold. The doors are open and at the librarian's desk presides a lady whom we will introduce as Mrs. Sampson. With her has come to the place of books a boy of six summers whose face gives unmistakable proofs of relationship that makes fit the name of John Peters, which she pronounces in her tenderly uttered injunction to the lad to "be quiet while mamma does her work, and perhaps grandpa will come to see us bye and bye." This librarian is none other than the daughter of Elder Peters, who, it will be remembered, was invited to Dayville nine years before, to see Miss Sampson the school teacher; but all mention concerning her has been crowded from this story by the other characters whom events have pressed into prominence. She became a friend of the teacher, her successor in the Dayville school, and finally her sister, Mrs. Albert Sampson. Walking thoughtfully up the granite pavement to the library is a young lady, evidently of not more than sixteen summers, but who seems to have the maturity of a woman of twenty. She is leading a little one of five years, who, pulling her hand and exclaiming, "See how bright it is!" holds up a leaf which she has picked from the pavement, and to the reply, "Yes, Marion, my jewel, take it home and papa will paint a picture of it for mamma," says "Won't that be nice!"

"And, my dear, I remember that when a child like you,

I played 'keep house' with my dolls here, in the shade of these very maples; and here, when I was grown a little older, the good Mr. Peters told· me the story of Jesus and His kind words to the little ones, that charmed me and led me to love the dear Christ!"

"And that's the same man that preached when mamma began to think about Jesus, isn't it?"

"Yes, Marion."

"And I'm going to love Jesus, too—I love Him now."

"Dear little one, I'll pray that the good Father up in heaven keep you safe all the time."

"Thank you—and wasn't you the little girl who carried the flowers to the meeting at the school-house? Mamma told me about it—how beautiful it was for you to think of it, and how naughty Mr. Barber the other minister was, who tried to throw the flowers out of the school-house and was stopped by Mr. Stedman. You see, Aunt Marion told mamma about it."

"Yes, Marion, I carried the flowers; and I remember how Mr. Peters asked me to forgive Mr. Barber for his rudeness, and I did forgive him. But often since then it has cost me a struggle to exercise a forgiving spirit."

"I'll try to be like you was then."

"Precious one! do you know, Marion, that that minister, Mr. Peters, kept right on preaching, and a great many people came to hear him, and now we have that pretty chapel up there for him to hold meetings in, right in the same place where the school-house stood in which the first meeting was held. On his way up to Hardland to preach, he used to drink from a spring flowing from the granite rocks by the roadside. He saved all he could of the little money he used to get for preaching and bought all those granite rocks. And from them pieces have been cut, with which the nice new town hall has been made, up there, on the corner across from the chapel. With the money that he had for the granite blocks he has bought the books that have been put up in the library here, for the folks to read."

"Isn't Mr. Peters good!—and isn't **God** good to give us such a man!"

"Yes, indeed, my little one."

In the library, Agnes Smith introduced—"Miss Marion Belmont Evartson; Master John Peters Sampson"—and turning to hide a smile at the charming manner in which the little folks stood regarding each other, received from the librarian the first book sent out from the institution. It was a copy of "Titcomb's Letters to Young People," of which work she had heard Doctor Robinson speak in high terms when at tea at the home of the Harrisons, where she was visiting. Going from the library and watching the little Marion as she ran along Main street until she had reached home, Agnes walked to the post-office at the store of the Dawsons, and found this letter, which she read as she leisurely strolled homeward:

"BOSTON, October 28, 1859.

MY OWN DEAR AGNES:—

We have had a most delightful journey, one that will be ever memorable to us both for the opportunities it has afforded us to see the works of nature and the achievements of man. And it will be especially dear to me for the revelations it has given me of the worth of him whom I have for years thought the noblest of earth and who now is mine forever!

Together we have gazed on the grandeur of the mountains of our native New England; together we have sailed the waters of its lakes, which excel, I am told, even the beauty of the lochs which mirrored the face of the fair Ellen that thrilled the bard of Abbotsford; together, to the rhythm of the waters of the Merrimac, we have floated seaward and in unison admired the Whittier who sings of that river! And here, at Boston, we have together noted with delight, the evidences of the prosperity of the good city; and here, and out at Concord and Lexington, we have together recalled the deeds and sacrifices of the fathers who won the freedom of this country and established its institutions!

And together we shall live, neither for self, but each for the other, he to do his work and I to keep his spirits in tune and his heart encouraged to do that work and do it grandly and well! O, how can a man without the enheartening of woman's words of love, work as becomes a man. And how few women know what a grand work and what a high mission is theirs! With the business before me of blessing the one whose I am and who is mine, will time hang heavy on my hands, and life become monotonous? and thus busied, will I need to fear that the one I am living to bless will become dictator? No, never! He will think me his benefactor. Such is my faith in him, and that faith will help him to be that which I believe him to be. Great indeed is the mission that is mine, and to fit me for it I shall need mental and spiritual growth, and shall seek it, and not only that, but shall ask the help and the guidance of the Divine Benignity! For reward I shall look into eyes that will tell of the gratitude and joy of a man who is all mine and not another's; mine for all time, with its struggles through which I shall help him, and not criticise him; its defeats, in which he shall have my sympathy, and its triumphs, in which I shall rejoice with him with joy unspeakable! And, mine he shall be in the experiences and the joys of the bright eternities! Agnes, those who say that matrimony is bondage know not of what they are speaking. It is liberty, it is queenship, it is heaven! And though the ceremony of making legal our union was only two weeks ago, as far as each heeding the wishes, hopes, and ambitions of the other is concerned we have been married five years, and I have a right to speak of matrimony! That ceremony is nothing of itself, we are married because mated! Marriage of mated souls is all I claim for it. The compelled living together of unmated souls, is bondage, is punishment, is hell! And now, with a husband to love enough to heed his wishes, and to hope for, and seek for his best good and the best success in life, shall I not, can I not, be as much of a friend to you as hitherto I have been? Can I not be more your friend then ever? And with all this joy that marriage brings, shall I not need your friendship as much as ever? Nay, I shall need it more, need it to give me the equipoise to help me to walk worthily with my joys. With you prizing me as possessor of those joys, I shall hope to feel increased obligation to hold them as the treasures they are.

Agnes, my friend, I have to thank your mother for many of the ideas which I have so freely told you, and for the example her life affords of an ideal love. With her near me I shall hope to live up to the standard I have adopted; but without the inspiration of her ways and words I should despair of so living. It will indeed be work, but work that I would like to do, and, in fact, hope to do in heaven. And, doing that work here, I shall have all the heaven that is possible for mortals on earth. Dayville and my good friends there will grow dearer to me with each passing year that carries me nearer to the heaven of the Beyond, whence I doubt not I shall look back with delight, and I hope with little regret, to this life below.

As I close this letter, Henry's kind eyes look up from his reading, and he sends you his regards. We shall soon return and of course we shall expect you at the reception; and come thereafter and always as often as you can, to see

Your friend,
MARION BELMONT JAMESON."

Agnes finished the letter as she reached home, and bestowing herself on an ottoman, and resting her arms on her mother's knee, she read the missive to her, and the father stood regarding the two, thinking, the while, doubtless, of an event of years before which then gave him joy and which was growing in beauty and significance with every year of the history of his life, the lives of those he loved, and .the life of the town that was growing up around them, an event that gave to the life of the people its upward trend, its sweetest flavor, its brightest horizon of hope!

Going to the garden, the good man returned with roses from the green-house, and, handing them to his wife and daughter, he said :—

"Elizabeth, I remember!"

"Yes, dearest, I remember!

Going to the library, Agnes gave her roses to Mrs. Sampson, and then went to the street and there soliloquized over the brook that so delighted her in other years: "I am glad the authorities have left it to run where it always has:

> 'Thou ever joyous rivulet
> Dost dimple, leap, and prattle yet,
> *   *   *   *
> The same sweet sounds are in my ear
> My early childhood used to hear!'"

"Dearest, said Mrs. Smith to her husband, when Agnes had gone, "how grateful should we be that our daughter is so sensible that we can trust her even with the fervor of such an ardent letter as that which Mrs. Jameson has written her. Many another girl would have kept the missive to herself instead of loyally bringing it to her parents and trustfully reading it to them."

Mr. Albert Sampson has for several years been doing a
thriving dry-goods business in the new Dayville where so
many families have come that Mr. Thompson, of Dayville centre, thinking there was room for still another
merchant, sold his stand at the old village at a sacrifice
and set up in business near the Dawsons, who gave up
their dry-goods department, Thompson returning the
compliment by confining himself to the dry-goods trade.
The Dawsons found groceries enough for them, and invited to the town a friend of theirs from New Hampshire,
to take their boot and shoe business to a new stand, where
he has found good patronage. A druggist has accepted
the invitation of Mr. Smith and begun business in his
line on the same street with the Dawsons, and is erecting
a house on a new way opened northward from Main
street, through the estate of the founder of Dayville and a
few rods east of his residence. This street, in honor of
the friend of whom the territory was purchased, has
been named " Williams avenue." A house has been built
there, which Mrs. Williams, on invitation of the Smiths, is
to occupy during her life, rent free, the arrangement being
that of the Smiths in remembrance of the kindness of Mr.
Williams to them when they were struggling to get a foot-
hold in the world. Other houses have also been erected
on the avenue and there Timothy Edgerley has selected a
site for a house wherein he proposes, some time, to install
his Jennie Davis. Eastward from the avenue to the
Hardland road extend two streets on which houses are

being erected by people who have been invited to locate
in the town and who have found themselves well pleased
with the surroundings there. Mr. Stedman, who continues in the management of the paper-making industry, by
the side of which other enterprises have been started, is
erecting at his leisure a residence west of the library
building and in the near vicinity of the home where,
in other days, the man of rude life was entertained as
he began the steps upward that have led him to social
eminence and business prosperity. Near the home of her
cousins, the Evartsons, is the house wherein Marion Belmont, as Mrs. Henry Jameson, is to preside, the home
which the talented and industrious young lawyer whose
name she bears has provided for her. He is to retain his
office at the county seat, and, in going between home and
business will avail himself of the facilities of the new railroad that has been extended from Wayfield, its first northern terminus, to Hardland, with prospect of still further
extension. In the vicinity of Jameson's house are more
new residences, with still others elsewhere in the growing
town ; and the Wayfield *News*, in noting the evidences of
the prosperity of the place, refers with excusable pride to
the " prediction of this journal which the improvement
already made leads us to think will soon be realized."

Meanwhile the old village has gone backward. Two
houses were burned a year ago, and the owners in cast-
ing about to prepare for rebuilding came to conclude they
had better locate in the " new part " of the town. Several

houses at the centre are tenantless from various causes. The blacksmith has let his fires go out and proposes to go elsewhere to begin business. The wagon-maker and tailor have gone to the New Light settlement, followed by the crispin of the deserted village. Eb Whitney undertook to keep the "liberty stable," but concluded it best to relinquish the undertaking. So many tipplers have died in late years that the business at the "tarvurn stand" has fallen off one-half. "Judge" Jones, the best "stand-by" of them all, held out longer than the rest, but there came a time when even he could not be counted on for patronage. For, the man "experiencing a change" through the instrumentality of Elder Peters, lived a sober life for a year before the death that came to relieve him from the great struggle he was obliged to maintain to keep his appetite in subjection. "Deacon Lem and Deacon Squint" still remain to second the Reverend Jonathan Edwards Barber in his ministrations. Jeremiah Joslyn still "continners" and faithfully bewails the "backslidings in Zion," and Bildad Beals still frequents the "assembly of the saints" of the standing order. But the doleful face he wears is in keeping with the decadence of the place where once he flourished, but where, now, with his "occupation gone" as deputy sheriff, he who won immortal honors as master of ceremonies at the double funeral of Dayville, is obliged to content himself with officiating at ordinary obsequies with only a dolorous dozen present and with seating such strangers as may chance to be at the old meeting-house of a Sunday. Is it a wonder that his boots have become too dispirited and listless to squeak above half their old-time vigor, and that Bildad himself has come to think that earthly glory is but a bauble and fame an illusion and a lie! His income as officer having ceased, he is obliged to "turn a penny" the best way he can, and so has taken the job of carrying the scant mail between the centre and the flag station a mile away, which station is all the accommodation the managers of the new road think the old village deserves, while they have established their principal station for all the region hard by the village of the once despised people who have a membership ot two hundred; and the whole population of a thousand fills their chapel to pulpit stairs and aisles, thus necessitating the enlargement for which preparations have begun. The old schoolhouse once standing there and which was removed to another location, has now given place to a finer and more commodious school building. It was only natural that Mrs. Smith should preserve as a relic the desk whereon her child placed the flowers for the first meeting of her order in the region.

CHAPTER IV.

THE MORLEYS.

THE Morleys were a noble race who had long dwelt at Wayfield, and who had long been identified with its interests and helpful to its growth in all that gave the town its social significance and its importance in the business world. Henry Morley, the founder of the family, who settled at Wayfield in the seventeenth century, was there represented two hundred years later, by a dozen of his descendants and by others in various parts of New England, many of whom returned annually to the ancient homestead, a mile out of the town on the Ridgeway road. In the "forties" many of those residing at Wayfield followed the "star of empire" and located in Ohio and farther west, leaving but two of their number in the town of their ancestors. One was David Morley, who remained at the old roof tree, and was fit custodian of the relics treasured there through the centuries of the family's history. The other was John Morley, who lived on an estate in the town on a street which had been named for his kindred, who had occupied the place for a hundred years. John Morley and his wife, who was one of the Ridgeways from the town of that name, had for years been prominent members of the Wayfield church and devoted

friends of its minister. Their son who died in his boyhood was long remembered as one of the brightest and
best of the little ones of the fold, and his sister, who lived
to grow up to be a strong and healthy woman, was as good
and as refined as she was vigorous in health. She was
the joy of the household, always helpful and always sunny
tempered, the best and the busiest of the teachers in the
Sunday-school, where all the children loved her; the de-
voutest and most consistent of the women of the Wayfield
church. And great was the grief of parents and fellow
disciples when they learned that Mary Morley was to be
married to the son of Allan Harrison, a man of atheistic
views who had for some years been a resident of the town,
and whose wife, Jeanie Murray Harrison, had like unbe-
lief in religion, while their son inherited the infidel notions of his parents. The Harrisons were people of
deserved excellent repute, and to the little wealth which
Mr. Harrison inherited they had added by years of econ-
omy and industry until they were possessors of an ample
fortune. Yet, in spite of their correct and pure life, they
were infidels, and their son was like unto them. So minister and deacons advised the young woman not to con-
summate the proposed alliance, and parents protested and
pleaded against it. But Mary Morley had a mind of her
own, and, when young Harrison, who was a beautiful
blending of the manliness of his father and the sweetness
and brightness of his mother, and whose two names of
Andrew Murray spoke the Scotch nativity of his ancestors,

had graduated from college and completed his term at the law school, he was married to the one he had chosen and the one he had promised to respect for her religiousness. Her father, who died soon after, and who had long before willed his estate to Mary, with the provision of a home for the mother with the daughter, had the good sense not to disinherit the latter for her disregard of the wishes of her parents in her marriage. And when, after adjusting her father's affairs, she came with her husband from the house of the Harrisons to her own home, she removed the name of her father from the door and with her own hand nailed in its place a plate bearing the name of the man who stood beside her, wondering at her act, admiring her bravery, and inspired with new love at the words—"Andrew Murray Harrison, I install you ruler of this mansion of the Morleys, custodian of their interests and protector of their good name. Andrew Murray, my own, you accept the trust?"

"Yes, Mary, dearest of earth; and in accepting the charge, I grant you, as before I promised, the fullest liberty of religious belief and life. Believe there is a God and that Jesus of Nazareth was divine. Devote a chamber as your place of orisons to heaven, and by the name you have pronounced to him who delights to bear it, he promises you that that place shall, because of the incense your prayerful soul sends to the skies, be sacred to your infidel husband forever."

And there Mary Morley Harrison offered petitions for

blessings on the poor and the needy, for grace to live, consistent with her professions and for heavenly influences to lead the one she loved to see the beauty of the character of the Christ and to become a follower of Him.

David Morley died a few years after his brother, leaving his son Edward and daughter Ida May possessors of the old homestead, and charged with the support of their mother and the care of the heir-looms in which the ancient mansion abounded. Among these treasures were military commissions bearing date a century or two previous and others of similar antiquity mentioning various Morleys as magistrates in the land. It was natural for the Morleys to be hospitable and that quality appropriately found its fullest and most frequent illustration in the original home of the race, where Ida Morley lived, whose joy and whose ambition was to do good, whose sympathies extended beyond her kinsfolk and acquaintances to the wants and woes of the poor of the parish and the town, and whose sentiments of kindness found frequent expression not only in words but in deeds. Herself and her cousin, Mrs. Harrison, rendered efficient aid to their minister in the charities of the church, and Doctor Robinson and his wife were frequent visitors at the Morley mansion, where the divine found not only helpful suggestions in reference to the poor of the congregation, but pleasant relief from his studies in the society of the Morleys and in looking over the antiquities which they treasured. He delighted to take an interest in the young men of his congregation, and there was scarcely one among them who had not good reason to believe that his minister was his friend. The manifestation of this interest he varied to suit the bent of each mind, and he could and did become companion of one on his angling bouts and the next day invite another to his study to discuss Hamlet or Hudibras, discoursing the day following with a young geologist and with him finding "sermons in stones," and, again, with still another, growing eloquent over flowers, the voice of a "running brook," or the carol of a bird. Extending his sympathies beyond his parish, he interested himself at one time or another in about every young man who came to the town. One of these was Edward Atherton, who, having completed the course at the Dayville school, sought higher educational advantages in a private school at Wayfield, and who accepted with gratitude the kindness of the minister. His genuineness so pleased his friend that he invited the young man to visit with him at the mansion of the Morleys, where he would receive that best of all helps in character building and polishing, the influence of people of refinement and intelligence, and be given opportunity to learn how to move with equipoise amid the appointments that culture selects for the homes of wealth. There he met Ida Morley, who, though yet young was so much his superior in years that she could be gracious to her visitor without giving occasion for the thought that she was inviting the behavior of a suitor. And what better blessing than this is there for a young man on earth, unless it

be the possession of a woman's heart? And what so fits
him to win that greatest good, and to worthily hold the
possession, as does this graciousness of an unselfish and
genuine woman! Such an one was Ida Morley. Doctor
Robinson had for years known that Miss Morley had a
great liking for poetry, and, good judge of it as he was, he
was delighted to find that she knew poetry when she saw
it. He had also discovered the poetic element in the
make-up of Edward Atherton. And pleasant indeed was
the scene in the parlors of the old house wherein the dig-
nified minister listened entranced to the voices of the
bright woman and her admiring friend, as they alternated
in reading the numbers of Bryant, and in giving passages
from the "Wizard of the North," or, as, with the three in
the shade of a beech, by a stream that sang its joyous
course through the grounds of the estate, the two vied
with each other to see which could, with Tennyson, best
imitate its babble :—

> " With many a curve my banks I fret,
>   By many a field and fallow,
> And many a fairy foreland set
>   With willow-weed and mallow.
>
>   *   *   *   *   *   *
>
> " I murmur under moon and stars
>   In brambly wildernesses;
> I linger by my shingly bars,
>   I loiter round my cresses.
>
> " And out again I curve and flow
>   To join the brimming river,

> For men may come and men may go,
> But I go on forever."

And his benign face serenely glowed as, to change the
scene, they sang, in beautiful blending of voices, Addison's "Firmament on high," and attempted the higher
grandeur of Cowper's hymn "God moves in a mysterious
way," or the heavenly sweetness of Wesley's "Jesus, lover
of my soul."

Doctor Robinson had, in a marked degree, the good
sense which kept him from being inquisitive and so made
him all the more welcome in the homes of his people. Not
only did he refrain from asking in words about matters
that did not concern him, but there was never an inter-
rogatory in his looks to prompt the suspicion that he
wished to know more than good taste permitted him.
And although it had long been to him a wonder that
Miss Morley had not encouraged the attentions of any
who sought her hand, he had never, by even a hint, asked
her reasons for this course, to say nothing of not advising a
different one. And when, in conversing upon ministers,
they chanced upon the New Light, Reverend Wilbur F.
Warren, whom the Wayfield pastor praised emphatically,
placing him next to Elder Peters, and Miss Morley discovered, in her words of assent to the doctor's liking for
the man, a warmth of admiration for him, the good minister's face gave no evidence that he noticed the inkling to
her interest, and she continued this praise until her words
were proof positive that she ardently admired the Wes-

leyan preacher. So, because of his lack of inquisitiveness, Doctor Robinson came into possession of a fact of great interest. And the news was in good keeping.

"I thoroughly like Mr. Warren," said Miss Morley, "for what he is and for what he preaches. His sermons are full of poetry. His utterances seem inspired, seem the words of one who looks into the other world and has an ear quick to hear the voices of those speaking from the realm of the spiritual."

"You are very right, my friend, and I am glad that I asked Mr. Warren to exchange with me ; glad because his discourses pleased you and others of the congregation and glad because inviting him showed our interest in the man. For he needs all the help that appreciation is, to nerve him for the struggle which he finds life to be."

"May I ask if there is anything of peculiar hardness in his lot in life ? "

"There certainly is, I am sorry to say. He is most unfortunately mated ; or, rather, he is not mated. For the one to whom he is legally bound is as unfit for the place which she nominally occupies as it is possible for a woman to be."

"How sad the fact ; I pity him, from my heart I do ! "

Ida Morley was gazing from the window as she said this, and Doctor Robinson, the uninquisitive man, assented to her statement and, with the art concealing art, turned the conversation. Had he learned something which his friend would not care to have divulged ? The secret was

safe with him.   So, evidently, she thought when returning
to him, with her mother, after an hour's absence, she
said :—

"Thinking of my emotions when we conversed concerning that minister, I want to ask your prayers that I remember the command against covetousness."

"Little does one of your generosity of heart and strength
of character need to make the request with which you
honor me.   But honor it is, and I'll heed it.   God bless
you, Ida May Morley!"

The stirring times of 1860 had come, and, knowing that
the welfare of their country was always a welcome theme
with the Morleys, their minister took up the subject,
dwelling with hearty emphasis of praise on the eloquent
addresses of Mr. Harrison in favor of keeping the territories sacred to freedom, whatever demand for more
room might be made by the slave power that had so long
dominated at Washington, influencing legislators and
shaping the policy of administration after administration.
"I fully agree with his ideas on the subject," said the divine, "and if, as he thinks it possible to happen in the
event of the election of Abraham Lincoln, the pro-slavery
people rebel, carry their states out of the union, and bring
on a war, I shall stand by the government!   And there'll
be thousands of brave young men to rally to the defence
of the old flag, and if the nation is compelled to the dread
arbitrament of arms, not only may slavery be kept from
the territories, but that pet institution, with which, under

the constitution, Congress has no right to interfere in the
states where it is already established, may be abolished,
as a war measure, by the executive as commander-in-chief
of the army and navy which the advocates of slavery have,
by their rebellion, compelled him to call into action."

"How well you have spoken," replied Mrs. Morley.

"Indeed you have," said Edward Morley, who, with his
wife and their little Katherine, had joined the group; "indeed you have. Cousin Harrison has done well, and it
was no small speech, that of Stedman's at Ridgeway, the
other evening. I shall hope, and pray, and vote for the
election of Abraham Lincoln !"

"Edward, my brother, you are right."

"I can pray, too"—and Katherine looked up to her
father and then to the minister who, saying, "My friends,
now is always the best time to do duty," arose and, lifting
his hands to heaven, petitioned the Throne for blessings
on the country !

"Doctor," said Edward Morley, when the minister was
leaving, "if the great emergency which you predict and
which we all hope may be averted, should come, remind
me of the promise which now I make to fight for home
and native land !"

"You'll not need reminding of such a promise, brave son
of the Morleys! But how terrible to think war is possible,
war between states that 'shoulder to shoulder went through
the Revolution !' and together rejoiced over the consumma-
tion of national independence ! Yet such is the awful por-

tent! The sky seems already darkening with the hate of the malcontents and we can almost hear the rumblings of the thunder of their wrath! their wrath who should be filled with gratitude to Heaven for so good a country and moved to patriotic devotion to the cause of the nation they seek to destroy!"

"How noble you are, and had your son lived he would have been ready to defend the government with his life."

"Ah, my noble Rowland! how he loved us, and how, boy though he was, he gloried in the valor and patriotism of the men of the Revolution!"

CHAPTER V.

WHEN the war cloud in the national sky burst on the land, the people of Wayfield were not surprised to find so patriotic a citizen and so discerning a man as their eminent lawyer fully aroused to the importance of the situation. With common consent they made him chairman of the initial war meeting in the memorable May days of 1861, and they listened with rapt attention to his fiery denunciation of the spirit of rebellion that had "prompted the attack on the flag of the country whose inhabitants are the most intelligently and most benignly governed of any of the peoples of earth!" Cheer on cheer testified the appreciation of his hearers, and with an eloquent appeal to his fellow citizens to "stand by the government of the grandest republic mentioned in the annals of nations! and uphold the hands of the executive of that republic, the noblest and most distinctive product of American civilization, Abraham Lincoln!" he urged the young men of Wayfield to "rally around the starry ensign of liberty and carry it through 'leaden rain and iron hail' and bristling steel, and plant it in triumph on the heights of the most impregnable stronghold of the enemy!"

Then supplementing his eloquence by writing in a clear, bold hand on an enlistment roll that unexpectedly to his

audience he produced on the spot, the well known signature of Andrew M. Harrison, he sat down amid tremen-
dous applause. Piety and patriotism are twin qualities of
the good man. And, quick on the beginning of quiet after
the outburst of patriotic feeling, arose the well-known
form of the New Light minister, who, saying, "A soldier
of the cross can serve the Master by fighting in defense of
his country," went forward and, though by his years·ex-
empted from compelled military duty, wrote on the enlistment roll that had been placed in charge of Henry Jameson at the secretary's table, the name of John Peters, second on the list whereon the third to be written was that
of Mr. Jameson. Mr. Harrison was on his feet again and
called up Dr. Robinson, who said :—

"Fellow citizens, they will not want a man of sixty in
the ranks, and I regret not only that advancing years will
prevent me from serving my country, but that I have no
son to represent me in the good cause that has so aroused
the hearts of the people I love. Most heartily do I commend the example of Elder Peters who, though ten years
my junior, is still beyond military age, and who, in spite
of his years has enlisted to fight for his country. If this
movement continues, as I hope it may, there'll be a regiment raised in this region. And who will be so fit for
chaplain of the legion as the pious and patriotic Reverend
John Peters, whom I now nominate for the place!"

"And all who favor the nomination," said Mr. Harrison, "will say aye!"

Close after the emphatic response in the affirmative, a young man, apparently about twenty years of age, arose in the audience and, saying to another near him, "The Robinsons shall be represented," walked to the front and wrote his name, when Doctor Robinson, arising, said: "Ladies and gentlemen, I introduce to you Carl Robinson, son of my brother, Judge Robinson, who has come from Yale to surprise his uncle with a visit, but whose exhibition of patriotism that has greatly pleased me has not surprised me, for it is like him, like his father and like his grandsire, who now at ninety years of age lingers in his ancestral home. Thence his father went forth, in the war of the Revolution, to fight the minions of the Georges, and to establish the liberty that is now imperiled by those who have grown up in the warmth and radiance of its sunshine, and who are bound by all the ties of patriotism to protect it with their 'lives, their fortunes and their sacred honor!'"

All eyes were turned, as a tall young man arose on whose earnest face determination was evident, and who, bending to listen to the words "Yes, Theodore, go and God bless you," that were calmly and sweetly spoken by a little woman near him, laid his hand tenderly on the head of a boy that was by her side, and saying, "Papa will be back soon, Teddy," walked forward and wrote, boldest among the signatures, the name of Theodore Cushman.

Springing to his feet amid the applause at Cushman's

act, the chairman said, as the signer was about to return to his seat :—

"There are noble qualities in that man's race. One of his ancestors was in the life guard of Washington and participated in the storming of Stony Point under the gallant 'Mad' Anthony Wayne. We have seen that this one of the Cushmans is patriotic and we all know he has talent for song. Shall we hear from him?"

"A song! a song!" was shouted from all sides, in response to which the patriot in his clear tenor voice gave "My country, 'tis of thee," and, "America" done, in answer to other calls, went grandly up to the culminations of "The Star Spangled Banner," at the close of which the enthusiasm of the people again showed itself in deafening cheers. Harrison, equal to every occasion, was again on his feet and called for more volunteers, closing his appeal with the first and the final stanza of Drake's "American Flag," emphasizing, with thrilling effect, the closing lines :—

"Where breathes the foe but falls before us,
With freedom's soul beneath our feet,
And freedom's banner streaming o'er us!"

As he finished his appeal, a dozen young men sprang to their feet and rapidly and with evident determination in their manner, went up and wrote their names below that of Mr. Cushman. They were members of his class in the Sunday-school of the Wayfield church, of the standing order, and were followed by others of that school.

Then, as a result of a whispered consultation between another of the teachers in the school and several of his learners, he and they came up to Mr. Jameson's table where the teacher wrote the name of Payson Sherwood, Jr., that was supplemented by the signs manual of his group, who were followed by still others. Trembling with emotion Deacon Sherwood arose and said :—

" Fellow citizens, proud that I am to be represented in the grand cause of our country's welfare by one bearing my name, and too old to enter the lists myself, I propose devoting to that cause something of the wealth that God has given me, and besides one thousand dollars which I offer as a fund to be put at interest for the benefit of the regiment or such of them as may return "—and the speaker's voice was melted to tenderness at the thought that some might never come back—" I propose to give one hundred dollars each for the families of any who may be willing to enlist and whose dependants may, on their going to war, have nothing for their support. This, and more will I do, if more is needed, for such as I have indicated, who may now enlist."

At this, Jake Sanders went deliberately to the table, and while he was writing his name the words, " And they are getting jail-birds to enlist, are they ? " from some one in the audience, were overheard on the platform by Mr. Harrison, who sprang to his feet and with the fire of indignation lighting his eyes, exclaimed :—

" Ladies and gentlemen, this insult to a man who, whatever may have been the misfortunes of his other days, has put between the experiences and sufferings of that time and the present, years of the most correct life, and who now reaches the climax of patriotism and manliness by offering himself on his country's altar, this cowardly insinuation from one whose own business transactions are at least peculiar, I denounce as most damnable! so despicable that it would be honored by the contempt of decent people!"

Then turning his eyes full on Lemuel Barnes from whom the words of interruption had come and pointing to him, the speaker said :—

" But, sir, we have with us that disciple of peace and love, Elder Peters, whom and whose doctrines you hate. I shall ask the people to copy the example of him who forgives every personal enemy, though he has enlisted to fight the enemies of his country; and if you, sir, will promise never to repeat your insult, we will overlook this impudence. I will also ask Mr. Sanders to accompany you to your carriage that you may suffer no violence. For there are those outside whose voices indicate that they have in meditation a more vigorous manner than ours of expressing their dissent from your ideas, of which they have learned by the unpatriotic utterances you have elsewhere made."

And accompanied by the man he had derided, the unpatriotic and cowardly man unmolested, sought his carriage and drove home!

There were still others to enlist, and it was half past nine o'clock when Mr. Harrison, to close the meeting, said :—

" Fellow citizens, rejoicing with you over the good work so well begun, and which we all fully believe has only begun, and thanking those who have offered their lives for their country and those who bravely give up their loved ones for that cause, and respecting those who believe in a divine power to whom human beings are responsible, and to whom for blessings from His hand, they should be grateful, I call on the Reverend Doctor Robinson for such petition, adoration, or thanks as he may be moved to address the skies."

And the Wayfield divine, lifting heavenward the hands that had so often been upraised in benediction and that always seemed designed to bestow blessings, thus voiced the emotions of the pious and patriotic people before him :—

" Thou God of nations and of men, Thou who rulest the armies of the heavens and who hast made, and who holdest to their orbits, the myriad worlds on high, but who deignest to care for the interests of the inhabitants of earth—

'O God, our help in ages past,
Our hope for years to come,
Our shelter from the stormy blast
And our eternal home !'

we come to Thee thanking Thee for the blessings which Thou hast granted this nation from the times of our forefathers unto these days, when all Thou hast given us of liberty and good government is imperiled by traitors ! We ask Thee to lead us through the troubles that are on us, through the Red sea of difficulty of war to the promised land of peace! And if, in this emergency, there is rebuke for the sin of human slavery, grant that there be true penitence for the crime, and that, in the prosecution of the war for the support of the government that has allowed the evil to exist, the wrong may be done away. Bless, we pray Thee, those who are to go to war and those who are to remain. Bless us every one and evermore. In Christ's name we ask and offer all. Amen!"

Mr. Jameson announced that a hundred names had been "inscribed on the roll of honor," and called for "Three times three cheers for the brave men and the flag they are to carry to victory!" The response came with heartiness; and from their first war meeting the people of Wayfield went home, thrilled with thoughts of patriotism and fully aroused to the momentous issue that had come upon the country.

The hundred was increased by fifty during the two succeeding days when those wishing to enlist called on Mr. Jameson at his office, and at subsequent meetings the volunteering continued until the number reached three hundred. And soon three companies went into camp at a place a mile out of the town, which, at the suggestion of Mr. Harrison, who had received orders from state headquarters to recruit a regiment, of which he was to be commander, was named "Camp Lincoln." And here he established the headquarters of the proposed regiment, to the nucleus of which, already in camp, came additions from neighboring towns. First among them, and organized and officered one day before the first of the Wayfield companies, was the "Dayville guards, Thomas Stedman captain commanding," who, by virtue of his seniority of rank was given the right of the line, while the right centre was held by the "Wayfield guards,' named in honor of the well-known militia company of the town, and containing many of its members, and of which new company the commander was Captain Theodore Cushman. Another of the Wayfield companies was commanded by Captain Payson Sherwood, Jr., while the "Ridgeway rifles, Charles Newton captain commanding," soon arrived from the town whose name they bore and to which town Captain Newton, who will be remembered as the Hardland deputy sheriff of years before, had removed in 1857, with Mary Sumner, whom he married a year previous. There was a boy of four summers, to whom, as he kissed him and his mother good bye, he said, "Sumner, your papa is going, with others, to drive off the bad men who are trying to destroy the country. He hopes to come back some time and he wants you to be good to mamma and to pray for papa that he be kept safe all the time." Then pressing the boy to his bosom as the wife and mother buckled the sword on her warrior husband, he kissed over and over again the dear ones, and placing the boy on his feet by his mother's side, again said "Good bye" and went out to the street in front of his house, where the "Rifles" were drawn up to receive him. Placing himself at their head, and lifting his cap to the two in the doorway, he drew his sword and gave the orders, "Attention, company! Right face! Forward march!" And soon they were hid from view by a turn in the road which led to the camp of their comrades in Wayfield.

Mrs. Newton went out to speak with her neighbors who had come to see their husbands, and brothers, and lovers, and sons depart for camp and to join with them in their sadness over the separation, their admiration for the bravery of the band, and their hopes that when the war was over they might see the loved faces once more ! Ah, those hopes ! which some of them were never to realize !

A company soon arrived from Hardland and vicinity in command, strange to say, of Deacon David Grout, whose eagerness for opportunity to exercise authority was by the hastily enlisted recruits mistaken for ability to rightly direct men and fitness for the place of honor and authority at their head. Still another company was enlisted at Wayfield and vicinity, while Ridgeway sent a second company three weeks after Captain Newton and his men marched to the rendezvous. And when the June roses bloomed there was a great day at Camp Lincoln.

At nine o'clock an officer of the regular army arrived from the state capital and to officers and men of the Wayfield legion standing in column of companies, with arms stacked, hands uplifted and heads uncovered, administered the oaths binding them for three years to the service of their country. At high noon the regiment and their friends from towns represented in the ranks partook of a bountiful repast, the gift of Deacon Sherwood. Grace was said by Chaplain Peters, and ladies of Wayfield and

Dayville served the viands. Gracing the feast an abundance of flowers spoke the interest of the Smiths in the
occasion and the taste of Agnes Smith, Mrs. Henry
Jameson and Miss Morley who arranged the beautiful
offerings. A national flag, the gift of Mrs. Smith, Mrs.
Claire Evartson, and others of the Dayville New Lights,
was presented the regiment, in a neat speech by Doctor
Robinson, to whom Colonel Harrison happily responded.
Captain Stedman was presented a sword, and Chaplain
Peters, in handing him the blade, remarked, " The members of the Sunday-school class of which you have been
teacher send, with this token of their good will, the promise
to pray that the God of battles protect the warrior with whom
and whose like they confidently leave the interests of their
beloved land!" And Stedman responded, "I thank you
and them and promise that, although surprised by my
friends, I will try to prevent surprises by the enemy."
Next came the presentation of a sword to Carl Robinson,
who had been chosen lieutenant in one of the Wayfield
companies, and whose attentions to Agnes Smith since
enlisting reminded people of a vacation visit of his
to Wayfield and Dayville, the year before. The tints of
her cheeks at mention of his name were unmistakable, especially to her rival lover Edward Atherton, who, a man
in the ranks and obliged to obey, seemed small in her eyes
in comparison with one who had the right to command.
In one less noble than Atherton this evidence of Robinson's success and his failure would have aroused jealousy

and anger; but he thought of the saying of an old book which he had often heard the New Light ministers quote to enjoin forgiveness of enemies. And, struggling with tears that spoke of humiliation greater than defeat in the field could be, he turned to Frank Dawson, a chum of his in the Dayville company, and said, "I am going to have a furlough to-night, to go up and see the Taylors; and I'll bring some roses and give to Lieutenant Robinson and at the same time kindly and politely say good-bye to Agnes, who will, of course, be near Robinson!"

The repast and its variations over, orders for the departure of the regiment on the morrow, for the seat of war, were read, signed "Andrew M. Harrison, colonel commanding; Henry Jameson, first lieutenant and adjutant."

The morning dawns with skies of serenest blue! And at the appointed hour each company marches with lively step from its street and takes its place on the ground used for parade, where the music plays tor them to form in line under the eye of Colonel Harrison. A few rods to the front of the "markers" he sits his chestnut charger finely, and at his right is Major John Walbridge, former sheriff of the county. At the left is Lieutenant-Colonel Ridgeway from West Point and from the town whose name he bears.

Most of the captains have in the few weeks of their military experience become skilled in handling their companies, and the parade is formed with but little need of interference by the adjutant. He notices, however, that one company is tardy in "dressing" to the line ; and in going to adjust the marred front he finds the delinquents to be the hundred who chose David Grout to command them and who already regret their choice, as is evident from several muttered "d—ns" which Jameson hears and which he well knows have no reference to himself. Returning to his post, he commands, "Troop, beat off," and the musicians with measured tread go down the front playing "Home, sweet home," when, after the regiment is briefly exercised in the manual of arms by the colonel, there is quick heeding of his orders—"Battalion, stack arms ! Right backward dress ! In place. rest !" And a roar of laughter greets a remark that is not down in the tactics, "One half-hour for farewells, and in the language of the noble Nelson, the country 'expects every man to do his duty !'" At the right of the line Harrison dismounts and lifting his hat, approaches a group of ladies who are in waiting to greet him and who surprise him with wreaths of roses. To this he responds with thanks for the gifts, saying, "Mrs. Harrison will be pleased with these remembrances." Again lifting his hat and saying, "Good-bye, ladies," he turns to spring to his saddle, but desists to hear from one who steps from the group. Pointing to a letter in one hand she says, "He writes that they have made him colonel, that the regiment starts next week for the scene of hostilities and that he wishes to be remembered to you." To this Harrison responds,

"Miss Davis, my compliments to Colonel Edgerley, with whom I shall be glad to meet the enemy," and mounting, he gracefully sails out the camp entrance and away to the home where one awaits his coming who seems to him the dearest of womankind. Her friends from whom he has just parted have not asked him why she was not with them.

One fond lingering embrace and kisses that mean volumes precede the heroic woman's words,—"My own, Heaven will protect you amid all the dangers of war; and, whate'er betide, we will be true to each other, and I know that you will be loyal to the old flag and that you will have a constant care for the welfare of the men of your command. Your interest in them will win their respect and inspire ready obedience to your orders. Remember me to Chaplain Peters, Captain Stedman and others whom I have met, not forgetting those who are in the ranks, especially Edward Atherton, to whom present my kind regards."

"That I will, dearest of the women of earth! Good-bye, angel one! Good-bye!"

"Hero, bravest, best! My own Andrew Murray Harrison, the protection of the Mightiest be round about you ever, and the Divine Benignity smile upon you and bring you back to me. Good-bye!"

On returning to camp, Colonel Harrison summoned Atherton from Stedman's company and in tones that could but inspire confidence and gratitude told the message of Mrs. Harrison, and, smiling graciously, lifted his hat as the soldier, saying "Thank you, thank you," touched his cap and walked away. Did the commander of a thousand men belittle himself by the unusual and unmilitary act of recognizing one of them? Did he not, rather, strengthen his hold on that man? And should the act become known to the regiment would not they take it as evidence of his quality and of his fitness to command? In truth, did not the consciousness that he had taken an interest in a private soldier and regarded him as a man, increase his ability to exercise authority with that firmness and equipoise which, of itself, inspires ready and gladly accorded obedience? "That Mary of mine!" soliloquized he—"her kindness to one of my men, will be worth everything to me in what it suggests. And the soldiers of the Thirteenth shall know that Andrew M. Harrison is their friend."

Agnes Smith, who responded coldly to Atherton's good-bye, spoken as she gave Lieutenant Robinson some roses, was so engaged with the attentions of the officer that she failed to notice the scene in which the man she was setting aside for one who had rank, received from the leader of the legion and from the first lady of Wayfield, words which would nerve him to the behavior entitling him to high honors, that sooner or later he would receive. And she did not notice that Miss Morley met him as he returned from the interview with the commander, and said to him, "Mother thinks it brave of you to enlist, and she has asked me to write to you, and we shall pray that God bless you."

"Thank you, Miss Morley," replied Atherton; and

touching his cap, he rejoined his company as the voice of
the leader called the regiment into line. Then following
the hearty response to the request of Captain Stedman for
" three times three for Camp Lincoln, the one for whom it
is named and the one who has there commanded," came
Harrison's orders, "Battalion, right face! Forward,
march!"

And the thousand of the Thirteenth leave their rendezvous and move through the streets of dear old Wayfield!
They are greeted on every hand with cheers and the dis-
play of the national colors from homes and from places of
trade, while school-children, distributed with teachers along
the line of march, shower them with roses, and arches of
evergreen and flowers are inscribed with such sentiments
as, "God bless our Defenders," "The Union forever," "Remember Baltimore!" A gala day it is indeed, but sadness
sobers the scene! "The bravest are the tenderest," and
the man who does not weep is the exception in all that
thousand! As the front of the column passes his residence
in Morley street, the leader lifts his hat to the lady sitting
at a window and revealing through the drapery festooning
the casement a face of rarest beauty, that speaks the spirit
of the heroine! Taking from her bosom a miniature like-
ness of the lord of her love, she presses it to her lips in
response to his salute, and then bows to acknowledge the
blades of Captain Stedman and other officers who recognize her as they march along. And there is special kindness in the smile and nod with which she receives the fare-

well that Atherton gives, as, in the ranks, he lifts his cap
and rejoices to think that he feels no discontent with his
humble station. The sergeant who gracefully dips his
colors is none other than Bill Jones. To his compliment
Mrs. Harrison bows graciously, and Jones remarks to
the man next to him in the color guard, "I say, Jake Sanders, an' its true ez preachin', that air Colonel Harrison
hez one ter hum thet's ez good ez he is, an' I hope ter all
thet's mighty thet he comes back safe agin frum the bizi-
ness we're gwine intew!"

"You're jes' right, sarge, an'here's what's a-gwine ter fol-
ler the colonel wherever he axes me."

"An', Jake, ef that air ole Graout gits a chance to boss
Atherton araoun' he'll be a-doin' on't. Seein' I'm one o'
Peters's sort I musn't tech Graout myself; but things'll
happen thet 'll pay the critter fer his cussedness."

"Bill, you're perdictin' sartin, an' I'll bet on't! An' I
.happened ter hear Atherton tellin' Frank Dorson what
kin' o' fine tork the kunnel telled him."

"Is that air so, Jake?"

"Yer ken bet yer pile an' orl yer ken borry." .

The soldiers have filled the train of fifteen cars in waiting for them at the station. And, lifting the silk in his
hand to signal the engineers of the two locomotives, the
conductor shouts, "All aboard!" and springs to the rear
platform where he gathers up the flowers rained at Colonel
Harrison, who is taking his farewell view of Wayfield, the

scene of his activities and achievements, and the home of his love !

Returning from Camp Lincoln, Mrs. Jameson called in Morley street, saying as she entered :—

" Dear Mrs. Harrison, how brave you are !"

" Thank you, Marion, it is so good of you to call. Stay as long as you can, this time, and come again, soon !"

" I can remain but a moment ; father is waiting outside for me, and baby will want to see his mother. He is six months old next week. He was a Christmas gift, you know."

"The precious one! kiss him a dozen times over for Auntie Harrison."

"That I will! Good-bye, noble one! And how I shall hope that Heaven protect him whom you have sent to the war to defend home and the dear old flag !"

" Good-bye, dearest, good-bye ! Yours is a great sacrifice, and I am glad the warrior I sent is to have so fit an associate as Henry Jameson."

" Dearest, how great the sacrifice you make to part, now, when you so much need him—to part *now* with the one you love !"

" Marion, dearest, come !"

And the two, clasped in an embrace which meant the sympathy that is beyond words to tell, were discovered a few moments after by Miss Davis, whose gentle coming marred not the scene into which she glided to complete the picture.

CHAPTER VI.

ARRIVING at New York at evening, the regiment pushed forward towards Baltimore, Washington and the front; but, obtaining permission from Colonel Harrison to absent themselves from the command at the metropolis for a day, Chaplain Peters and Captain Stedman tarried there, the one to purchase a library for a Sunday school of the New Lights that had just been established on the Wayfield district, and the other to complete important business transactions that he had previously begun for the corporation of which he was agent. The next day, the objects of their tarrying done, they sought a dining place with which Stedman had become so familiar on previous visits to the city that he now entered without noticing the change of name on the sign. A man with a strange face was occupying the desk, and for him Stedman at once conceived a strong dislike that rendered it easy for him to believe the revelation of the scene which began to be enacted soon after, when he heard the following slowly stated utterance :—

"Thee can beg this young woman's pardon."

And looking up from his dish, the officer saw a man in Quaker dress in front of the desk, and near him a woman whose service garb was in striking contrast to the delicate hand extended to the counter's edge, as if in support of the frame that was a-tremble with fear, and to the fine face speaking in its lineaments much character, a lovely disposition and a high soul, and mantled now with mingled indignation and anxiety, but with rifts in the clouds revealing glimpses of hope inspired by the friendly interference of a Friend.

Concluding his demand, the man in drab took up a business card as the fellow addressed replied :—

"I hain't goün' ter beg no gal's pard'n what works fer me, fer anythun' I say ter her."

"James Van Bromp, thee will now beg this young woman's pardon, or thee will settle for thy bad words as a judge tells thee, and the case will be given at once to a young lawyer in the next street who will believe Ezekiel Slayton against a dozen like thee."

An apology was stammered out, the woman went back to her work and the Quaker resumed his place at a table where a sombre-dressed young woman said in a whisper :—

"Thee did well, father, to make that rude man heed thee ; but will not he, when we are gone, be all the bolder with his wrong words to the woman ?"

"Hannah, thee is right, and I thought of it when——"

"Will you please read this note ?" said the befriended woman, as, in returning from the cook-room with an order, she passed the table of the Quakers.

Perusing the penciled scrap of paper which ran, "I thank you, Mr. Slayton; but it will be all the worse for me

when you go. What shall I do?" the Friend, saying,
"Hannah, thee please finish thy food and be ready to act
as I ask thee," went to the table where his protegé had
deposited her waiter, and, the two moving a few steps
from the table, he said to her :—

"Tell me thy name, if thee please, and how thee came
here."

"I am Lillie J. Ten Eyck from York state, where my
father is a man of means and high standing. My mother,
who was a Johnson from Dayville in New England, died
several years ago. Father's second wife dislikes me and
I came here to learn how to work. The former owner of
this business, was from our town, and from the neighborhood of father's "Creek-side" estate, and is a worthy man.
He sold the place last week. This fellow, I fear, is what
you might think from the words which you rebuked him
for using."

"Thee tells an honest story, Lillie, and would thee like
to go with my daughter Hannah and myself to Pennsylvania, to live and perhaps teach in a Friend's school?"

"Yes, I thank you."

"Come with me—" and at the desk the Quaker demanded :—

"Thee will pay this woman her wages."

A gruff demurrer from the one commanded brought this
response :—

"Thee will pay what thee owes—that young lawyer
would like the work of suing thee. And I think the man

yonder with fine war clothes, who is looking this way, would like to go and tell the attorney to come."

Overhearing the words of the Friend, the officer left his lunch and approached the desk, saying :—

" Mr. Slayton—for I believe that is your name—I am Thomas Stedman from Dayville in New England. Chaplain Peters and I have stopped over here and we are to go by the train, two hours hence, to Philadelphia, and thence push forward to join our regiment at the front. What can I do for you before that time ? "

" Nothing, I thank thee," said Slayton, as Van Bromp counted out the money demanded.

" This is my friend Chaplain Peters," said Stedman, as his associate came up, " he is one of the New Light ministers, and proposes to pray for us who are going to thrash the rebellion out of those secessionists."

" The Friends think well of the New Lights for their sober-mindedness, simplicity and what they call 'leadings of the Spirit.' Thee is welcome to the good will of Ezekiel Slayton. And if thee could come out to the settlement where he lives he would like it very well. He wishes thee health and peace and much sparing of thee from harm by the shots of those who begun this bad war, which he hopes the men like thee and thy friend Stedman will stop."

There needs no detailed account of the trip of the Slayton party to Philadelphia and needs no saying that in the same coach with them journeyed the two men in uniform,

the eldest of whom was invited by the Broadbrim to sit
with him and tell him "more about the New Lights," while
the younger one wearing "war clothes" was introduced to
Lillie Ten Eyck and the Quakeress who were further back
in the coach. Wasn't it difficult for Slayton to conceal
the fact that there was another reason than the one he
alleged, when, a few moments out on the trip, he asked his
daughter to "come forward and hear what Mr. Peters has
to say to us about his kind of meeting."

Lillie Ten Eyck thought but half an hour had elapsed
when the train "slowed up," as trains will do when ap-
proaching a principal station, grandly and quickly coming
to a complete stand-still, instead of disdainfully granting
the brief half moment of halting to which "Huckleberry
Run Crossing" is entitled. Surprise and regret were on
the face that looked up when Hannah Slayton said, "Thee
will have to leave him now, Lillie. And I want to say
farewell to thee, Friend Stedman, and that I hope thee
will not get hurt where thee is going."

"Good-bye, Miss Slayton," said the officer, as the Quakeress withdrew to give her farewell to Chaplain Peters
and join her father, who had alighted.

Captain Stedman was conscious that the woman he had
met admired him, and pressing warmly the hand that was
placed confidingly in his, he said :—

"Miss Ten Eyck, I think woman's words would seem
dear to a man away from home and surrounded by the
dangers of war, and would help him to resist the demoral-

izing influences that must attach to army life even when at its best. And if you wish to write in reply to letters from me, the promise so to do I shall prize highly, and by worthy behavior before the enemy I will show my appreciation of the honor conferred."

"The honor you show me, sir, given with the frankness and sincerity which greatly enhance its worth, I shall be glad to accept; and I hope the God of battles will protect from harm the one I can but respect and that He will make mighty for the defense of the flag of our country the blade wielded by this hand which I clasp and say, good-bye!"

And in a trice Miss Ten Eyck was out the coach, while, recalling the fact that he had not learned the address of her Quaker benefactor, Stedman stepped from the coach and asked him, and, springing back to the platform of the car as the train began to move, heard him say, "Ezekiel Slayton, Cohecton, Pennsylvania," which words the officer noted in his memorandum book as he seated himself by Mr. Peters. While correct habits and the consequent serenity of mind made the chaplain so good a sleeper that to be broken of one night's rest disturbed him but little, the second sleepless night told on him. The night before leaving camp he had watched with a sick man who was a member of the church of the New Lights at Ridgeway, and a fire next the hotel in New York broke him of his rest, while Captain Stedman slept soundly through the excitement caused by the burning and never felt more wakeful

than he now did, on the lovely June evening of his journey southward. His friend was soon sleeping, and Stedman, who had noticed some ill-visaged fellows board the
car at one of the stops, and others joining them who had
come on his train, was seated where he had the crowd and
the chaplain in full view, while a slouch hat drawn down
over his face and the limp left hand that hung by his side
made to appear real the sleep he was feigning. And he
was not only awake, but believer in impressions as, by his
associating with his minister, he had become, he kept his
right hand on his pistol, ready to act in whatever emergency might arise to substantiate the apprehension which
came to him when the new passengers entered. Watching every movement and listening he heard one of the
roughs whisper :—

"I say, Jack Van Bromp, when's Jim, yer brother,
a-goün' ter start 'tother kind o' bizniss up ter N'Yawk?
That's a mighty fine gal o' hisen, that—let's see, what's
the name he telled me?—Ten Eyck, yes, I reckon that's
it."

"G'lang with your purty gals now; we're in for 'blood',
yer know; an' jes' see them too sojer duffers sleepun'.
Purty sojers them be! Ain' see the one nighest ter us
haiz a watch thet we can git. Step back kainder sly, Bill,
ain' keep the big feller from movun', uf he should wake,
ain' I 'll yank the ticker, ain', next stop, we'll vamoose."

"Not much!" thundered Stedman, as he sprang and,
with his left hand knocking the Bill aforesaid, flat in the

aisle, held his pistol full in the face of Van Bromp and
with his left hand dropped one after the other of the rest
of the gang as they came up. The train had now reached
the stop. The conductor, who had strangely refrained from
interfering with the roughs, allowed them to "vamoose",
and as the train progressed, quiet was restored among the
passengers who had been aroused by the scene enacted.
And Stedman and Peters, without further unpleasant incident by the way, reached their command the next evening
and were received with the most cordial feeling of comradeship by officers and men. This was a fair specimen
of the good will that, with very few cases to contrast, obtained throughout the regiment and which augured well
for its success in the mission whereto it was sent. For,
as in no organization is inharmony so disastrous as it is
in a body of troops, in no organization does harmony
among the members give such effectiveness in the prosecution of the work to which it is summoned as it does in a
military command. Harmonious among themselves, a
body of soldiers is likely to produce discord among their
foes. An army united has its best fitting to divide and
defeat the enemy it opposes.

In referring, in a conversation with the chaplain, to their
episode with the roughs, Stedman said to Peters :—

"Had we not been so far out of New England I should
have ·thought that the last one of the fellows whom I·
floored in that train was Sam Simpkins."

"There was a resemblance."

Peters, who, as chaplain, was in charge of the mail of the regiment, had other reasons than those arising from his position, for taking good care of the letters sent and received by Stedman ; for that officer had made a confidant of him in reference to the acquaintance with Miss Ten-Eyck. And the minister exceeded the obligations of office and of friendship as well. In a conversation which he planned so adroitly that it seemed unplanned, he drew from Surgeon Johnson the remark, that, " My cousin's daughter, Lillie Ten Eyck is the whitest soul living— Heaven bless the girl." These words, it is needless to say, the chaplain took occasion to repeat to Stedman, who, found it easy to believe them. The chaplain never asked and never knew whether Stedman mentioned the compliment in writing to his friend; and it was not until long after, that Stedman learned of the compliment given him by Mrs. Smith, in reply to a letter of inquiry from the Slaytons concerning him.

Returning from Camp Lincoln, Mrs. Smith retired to the parlor; and, kneeling where often she had prayed, the good woman besought the Heavenly Father for "courage to act, and wisdom to act rightly." Coming to the living room as Agnes entered, who had driven from Wayfield with Mrs. Jameson and her father, the mother greeted her daughter with more than her wonted tenderness, affection that brought the reciprocation which was proof that filial love was strong enough to lead the girl to patiently endure,

if not kindly receive, criticism of the behavior prompted
by that passion which to the young, enraptured by it, seems
the embodiment of wisdom, or, rather, seems to transcend
the highest wisdom. Where the one had prayed, the two
bowed a few moments in silent prayer, and, arising, the
mother who was, as every mother should be, companion
and confidant of her daughter, said, with a great depth of
tenderness in the utterance : —

"Agnes, I love you! May I speak?"

"Of course, mother."

"It is concerning what I have seen to-day."

"You think I ought to prize Edward Atherton more
than I do Carl Robinson, who has done something in his
student life for which he has been given a place wherein
he will be recognized as a gentleman. And shall Agnes
Smith refuse to recognize, admire and love this suitor, and
in his place accept the one who has gained no position
in which he would be regarded a gentleman?"

"But," said Mrs. Smith, "seeing you mention names
and institute comparisons, Edward Atherton *is* a gentleman, if he is in the ranks. And, granting that Robinson's
commission came as recognition of his industry as a student, did it not also come, and perhaps largely, as a compliment to his father and his uncle? And, Agnes, who
knows but Edward Atherton may do something that is
brave and that will win him a name and a place? Or,
better, who knows but he will do something that will give
him developement and growth and so make him worthy of

promotion, whether he receives it or not?"

"Yes, mother, and, to emphasize my liking for Robinson, I treated Edward Atherton almost discourteously when I should have been kind to him, acquaintance and school-mate as he was, and about leaving home to enter the hard-ships of army life."

"Your better self is speaking, Agnes, and if you care to refer to this matter again, my daughter, do so to-morrow.

As Agnes came down to the living room the next day, she said, as she greeted her mother with a cheery "Good morning," in which there was, however, evidence that she was in a thoughtful and sober mood : —

"You were right in your remarks concerning Mr. Ather-ton, and if he really has the nature which you attribute to him, how keenly he must feel the fact that, by inexorable military custom he will be kept from associating with those who are held to be gentlemen, and the fact that he will also be compelled to associate with those who, by the dic-tates of the same military fashion, are not regarded as gentlemen, and the quality, or lack of quality, of some of whom makes them to be the ignobles they are thought to be, and renders it degrading to associate with them ; while it will be almost a miracle of wise behavior to hold him-self above any of them without incurring their dislike or positive hatred."

"You seem to understand the customs obtaining in military circles. Yet I think things will be different in the Thirteenth; that it will be just like Colonel Harrison to

appreciate men for their worth rather than for the place
they occupy. And he will 'set the style' for the other
officers of the regiment. From his own promptings he
will be thus democratic and just in his ways, and his regard for Mrs Harrison, who, I hear, has a high regard for
the men in the ranks, will lead in the same direction."

"Marion told me, as we were driving from Wayfield,
that Mrs. Harrison sent a kind message to Edward by the
colonel, who did the errand, adding his own indorsement.
And Marion said that, in thanking his commander, Atherton showed the politeness which only one of fine instincts
exhibits. You see, Mr. Jameson as adjutant, was near
his chief when the scene occurred.

" Beautiful, indeed, was it not? And think how highly
one like Atherton would appreciate a woman's kindness,
a woman's friendship—I go not so far as to say a woman's
love! Like others from this region, Atherton has gone,
determined to live above the degrading associations of
army life with which he must be surrounded. And your
acquaintance with him gives you the right, the high privilege, to manifest that interest which shall help to keep him
to that determination. You are invited, by the fact of
your acquaintance, to inspire him so to behave amid, and
through, and against, the dangers and demoralizing scenes
incident to military campaigns, that he shall be broadened
and strengthened in character by that behavior, and, sur-
viving the hard experiences, shall return to thank you for
your interest in his welfare, or, dying, shall bequeath to

you the precious legacy of the right to think that you aided him to become the noble man he was, and bravely to give the precious offering of his life for his country— fit theme for harp of loftiest song!—heroism calling forth the gratitude of his countrymen and challenging the admiration of the skies!"

"And in inviting the attentions of one who had place, and largely, I must confess, because he had place, I have been selfish, when Edward Atherton, without thought of place or honors, has been unselfish enough to give everything, and brave enough to risk even life itself, for his country! Can a woman afford to be selfish when man is brave? Yet, not only was I selfish in my favors to Lieutenant Robinson, but accompanied the smiles in that direction with coldness and even rudeness to Atherton, to whom, I should at least have been courteous. Instead, scarcely did I recognize his polite words of farewell spoken to me when he came to present some roses to the officer, who, as he could but see, was supplanting him in my regard. Did even Elder Peters himself ever better illustrate the beautiful doctrine of forgiving one's enemy than did Edward Atherton in his generosity to his rival!"

Agnes Smith, kneeling, sobbed by her mother, in genuine repentance. And when, from a communication of the commander of the Dayville company to her parents, she learned the whereabouts of the Wayfield legion, she wrote a letter to "Mr. Edward Atherton, Care of Captain Thomas Stedman, Company A. Thirteenth Regiment."

And Mr. Dawson at the post-office, who noted that the missive was superscribed in her handwriting, tossed it, as if to ascertain its weight before placing it on the letter scale, or as if a letter of the importance that he divined this one to have was entitled to the ceremony of two weighings. He soliloquized thus, when Mr. Smith who had deposited it, handed him the requisite second stamp and departed: "A large letter, that which Agnes has sent; an' I'm mighty glad on't, for she's a mighty fine girl, an' Edward's a great sight smarter an' better th'n Carl Robi'son, if he is leftenant." But he knew not the sincerity of penitence, the heartiness of friendship, the cheeriness of encouragement with which the letter was freighted.

The chaplain in his rounds of distributing the mail of the regiment, delivered Atherton the missive at an outpost where he and Frank Dawson were on picket with others. And the two went from their comrades to a spring a few rods distant, and threw themselves, soldier-like, on the slope, under the pines that shaded the fountain, where Atherton held up the letter, saying, "Dawson, you know the handwriting of that address, you worked so long in the post-office at Dayville."

"From Agnes Smith! And here's lots o' good wishes for you and the girl that's sensible enough to think a fellow like you is worth noticing, if he doesn't wear shoulder straps."

September found the Thirteenth in fairly good condition, for a regiment that had seen the fighting which had been the lot of this legion. The officers and men were in good health and spirits; the last of those wounded at Bull Run had returned from the hospital "eager for the fray," and every day gave Colonel Harrison new evidence of the loyalty of his command to their leader and to the cause in which they were enlisted. But his face had for some time worn unmistakeable looks of anxiety. If any questioned the cause of this concern Adjutant Jameson and Chaplain Peters did not. And when, as, at the close of an afternoon parade, they were sitting at headquarters, a messenger from the nearest telegraph station approached, and, dismounting, handed Harrison a dispatch, his associates watched his face with interest and were delighted to see the cloud dispelled by a smile of joy. Handing the message to the chaplain, the commander drew his note-book and penciled a reply, and Peters read to the adjutant this enheartening announcement to their chieftain :—

"WAYFIELD, September 10, 1861.

DEAREST, MINE :—

Andrew Murray Harrison, Junior, who arrived yesterday, sends hearty greeting to his warrior father in the field; and with prayers for your safety, for the welfare of the regiment, and for the success of the cause in which the Thirteenth is enlisted, I am,

Always your own,

MARY."

The horseman galloped away bearing the words :—

"IN THE FIELD, September 11, 1861.

DEAREST MARY :—

With your caress, bestow on the boy, for his father, the heartiest kiss of parental love and when you are strong enough carry the number to a hundred, and as far beyond as you choose. This commission from one who declares you greater treasure than all the wealth "of Ormus and of Ind," and who deems himself possessor of greater honors than martial glory or imperial power, in that he has the right to subscribe himself,

Always your own,
ANDREW MURRAY HARRISON."

"Jameson," said the colonel, "tell Stedman, Cushman, and the rest they are wanted at headquarters." And as those officers and others came, Harrison said :—

"Gentlemen, there's an event in Morley street of Way-field, which I propose to celebrate in a manner that will be especially pleasing to the mother of the young man whom she has named for his father. It is her idea that the common soldier is a very important part of an army, and in compliment to her, I propose treating every member of the guard of the Thirteenth for September 11, with hot coffee that will keep them awake on their rounds and oranges, that, in anticipation of the event we celebrate, I have in waiting in the box yonder, which, Jameson, procede to break open. Then summon the best cooks and tell them to make ready for forty.

And the commander went the rounds of the camp lines, responding to the "Halt, who goes there?" of the sentinels, with "Friends with the countersign, and coffee!" to which the response came in keeping with the merry mood of the colonel, "Advance, friends, and give us both." When Harrison and his party neared the path paced by Atherton, who happened to be on guard that night, they noticed that Captain Grout, who was officer of the day, was trying to "test" the sentinel. He had slyly approached Atherton with the hope of surprising him and was trying, by coaxing, and then by commanding, to take his piece from him, but the guard persistently and successfully refused to part with the gun. As Grout departed, Harrison, without noticing that officer, approached, and, answering the challenge of the sentinel, said, "Atherton, I am right glad to see you and to know that you understood your duty. Mrs. Harrison has sent me news to day that pleases me, and I have come out to see the boys and give them something to break the monotony of their vigils."

Though Grout had exceeded his duty, Harrison did not interfere, and that refraining which the captain ought to have taken as forbearance on the part of his superior, rather than as proof of the colonel's approval, he seemed to regard as an indication that he could continue such annoyance of the guards without stricture. So he proceeded to the opposite side of the camp where he similarly "tested" Dawson, whom he could not get to give up his gun. At parade the next afternoon Atherton appeared wearing the chevrons of a sergeant, and Dawson decked with the stripes of a corporal, Atherton having been given the higher place because of his generosity to his comrade in demanding that the latter be made sergeant.

"There, mother, " said Agnes Smith, as, from a letter of Captain Stedman, to her parents, she read that officer's comment on the unselfishness of his soldier, "its just like Edward, is'nt it?   And I'm so glad, mother, that you insisted that———and that———."

"Yes, Agnes, I understand."

On a beautiful moonlight night in 1862, there was an episode in the army life of Captain Stedman that not only proved true his surmise concerning one of the fellows he encountered on the train on his journey southward, the year before, but that came near resulting through that man's instrumentality, in his incarceration under circumstances that would have insured a long detention, under the most rigorous and humiliating surveillance.   Among the camp followers of the brigade including the Thirteenth, was an evil-eyed adventurer, who, while appearing occasionally as sutler's helper with some other one of the regiments, kept well out of the one wherein he would have been likely to be identified.   He had, however, once or twice, visited the camp of that command, and on the morning preceding the night in question, when Captain Stedman was officer of the day, he made his appearance there, and was seen to walk outside the lines accompanied by Captain Grout, who, having just been officer of the day, was entitled to be off duty.   He soon returned to camp from the opposite side, and he came minus the other man, a fact of which no one, however, took note.   The quartermaster, who saw the fellow depart with the officer, did not suspect the man of being the thief who, the night before, carried off the half dozen uniforms which he had just now discovered to be missing from his store of supplies.

The brigade held the front, and the Thirteenth, pushed farthest forward, picketed the outposts. Stedman, accompanied by two soldiers, was making, that night, his first round of the picket lines, and neared a group of six at the end of a stretch of pines. The number was unusual for a picket guard of one post, but clad in blue, that was plainly discernible in the moonlight, and, sentinel-like, challenging his approach, they awakened, by their numbers, no suspicion of foul play; and the denouement they had planned they now sprang upon him. One of the accompanying guard, in answer to the challenge of the rebels who had assumed the role of federal pickets, went up and gave the countersign and with the routine words, "Countersign correct—advance, friends," Stedman and the other soldier approached, when the three found themselves sprawling on the ground and their mouths gagged to prevent outcries. Then, lifted to their feet, they were rushed forward under cover of the pines, half a mile, to the outermost of the rebel pickets, who being advised of the plot, allowed approach without halting. And the kidnapers, with their victims bound hand to hand, were made ready to march with additional guard back to headquarters of the regiment that held the advance of the rebel army. As they were about starting, one of the captors said, as he eyed the captain, "Tom Stedman, yer'll stan' a right smart chance o' gittun' to Andersonville when Pinckney gits his

eye on yer, yer d——d Yank," an opinion which, when
Stedman arrived at Pinckney's camp, he thought fully warranted. There he was greeted by the well remembered
Simpkins, who laughed in fiendish glee, "Ha! ha! Tom
Stedman, yer remember when yer got some one inter jail up
ter Wayfield, hey? How do yer like it now, yer d——d
son-of-a-gun! Where's yer Elder Peters now? How'd he
dew ter pray yer out er this? I was on that air train an'
hearn yer honey tork tew that air Ten Eyck gal." And
the man shook his fist in the face of Stedman as he closed
his taunts and was greeted with, "Well yer d——d Yank
yer did tell the truth, didn't yer, but I reckon yer'd a right
smart more like ter tell a lie, ef 'twould pay as well."

This eulogy done, a burly fellow, with sinister eye, and
shoulders crowned with the straps of a colonel, approached
Stedman, saying, "Ha! ha! yer d——d over-grown Yank,
how'll Lillie Ten Eyck, like this? Write yer purtiest to
the lady givun' her the compliments of Phil Pinckney, him
that she soured on, that summer up at Creek-side, and
then took up with such a dog-goned blasted Yankee whelp.
Yer G—d d——d big aberlitionist, I'll have my niggers
dance the devil's hornpipe round your carcass! Ha! ha!
D—n ye, not so easy as that, fer yer'll take a jaunt across
caintry to Bob Toombs's tavern, ter Andersonville, where
yer'll be kept till Lill Ten Eyck cries her eyes out and goes
inter hur grave. Ah! you d——d Yank, ain't yer grateful fer the consurlation?"

And the brute officer turned to the kidnapers, who, had

doffed their blue garb, and clad in butternut, appeared before him, as if in waiting for something. "Thar's hog and
hominy waitun' fer yer at the cook house over yon," said he,
"ain' yer'll fin' a keg o' apple jack not more'n half drunk
up, at headquarters, where I'll be, right soon after I git
'tothers started with this ere d——d Yank for Andersonville.

During these insults Stedman had remained quiet, and
as Pinckney left him he bowed his head and silently petitioned for aid of Him whom he had learned to trust, and
who, even now, in this most terrible emergency of his life,
he had faith to believe would not desert him.

Chaplain Peters, questioned, without doubting, the meaning of the voice within, that at midnight aroused him and
bade him go beyond the outposts, and, in a place to be
designated, pray for God's blessing on some one whose
name was there to be told him. "Not disobedient unto
the heavenly vision," he went forth, praying silently, "Lord,
guide and protect." Colonel Harrison always entrusted
him with the countersign, and he passed the camp guard,
and the inner and outer picket posts, and, though warned
that it would be dangerous going outside the lines, kept on
until he reached a pine copse, twenty rods to the right of
the belt of pines which the kidnapers had planned to use
as a cover for their retreat. Here he knelt, and silently
prayed, "Will the good Lord bless and protect Captain
Stedman. Keep him, dear Lord, from harm." Then, in
the intensity of his anxiety, prone upon the earth, the man
of God prayed, with faith still triumphant over fears,

"Lord, bless—and, O Lord, Thou wilt bless!" Listening, he heard the tramp of horsemen, and saw them halt and tether their steeds at the outer picket post of the enemy, and then go toward the federal camp. Remaining quiet until they returned, he heard, borne on the air, the prediction in reference to Stedman's destination. The capture, so adroitly done, that it was not even suspected by the Union pickets, was thus, through the faithfulness of Chaplain Peters to his favorite idea, known to him. And before the prisoner was started southward, the man of ken, passing the pickets, whom he informed what had happened, and enjoined to keep silent as he would break the news at headquarters, was at his colonel's tent, where, he gently shook the officer, and told the happening.

Springing from his blankets, Harrison roused his adjutant with, "For God's sake, Jameson, they've captured Stedman! Alarm the camp! No—let's have the scoundrels think we know nothing about it."

"All right, colonel; and Peters, you say, is sure they're going to take him to Andersonville?"

"Yes; and that same Peters, with his notion of the voice within is better than all our sentinels—excuse me, chaplain, for being personal."

"And I know," continued Jameson, "that Major Tompkins of the cavalry squadron of our brigade must have some fellows who'd like to give the Johnnies a chase, and bring back the prize they have captured."

"Call Tompkins."

And the cavalry major soon appeared, saying, "Yes Harrison, I have your man, good as gold, true as steel, and ready to meet the devil himself, cool as a judge, and quick as lighting—Lieutenant Clinton. And he has forty fellows in company L who are aching for a tilt, and equal to the most hazardous exploit."

Peters retired to his tent to give thanks for the results thus far of his heeding the call of duty, and to pray that the party sent to the rescue might be successful. Clinton, summoned and informed what was wanted of him, said, as he appeared before Colonel Harrison :—

"What, Stedman captured! And I'll be blamed if I don't think he's fallen into the hands of that confounded Pinckney! for I was told by a Johnny whom some of my fellows captured, that Pinckney was commanding the rebel advance in our front. He used ter hang aroun' our village in York state, and was given the slip by old man Ten Eyck's daughter, and everybody liked her for it, including Henry Clinton, that once she mittened, and who allows she served him right because he left her for another. And yet 'twas a slap in the face to Henry Clinton all the same. But he vows to goodness that he'll pay her off by gettun' back Tom Stedman fer her. The fact is, Elder Peters, that chaplain o' yours, has got me, an' I promised him, the other day, that I'd begin a new life an" in keepun' with that promise,'would forgive those who had wronged me. So I'd like to rescue Miss Ten Eyck's friend for her. You see, since our squadron's been with the brigade I've struck up a likun' fer Stedman, an' he's told me of his friendship for the lady. An', to tell the truth, colonel, I ain't sorry for the way that affair terminated, as Katrina Van Hoosen well knows, that now swears by a fellow about my size an' delights to bear his name. In five minutes, Harrison, I'll be here with forty of the bravest that ever drew sabre and that are longun' for a brush with the enemy."

"All right, lieutenant, and I shall await with expectancy the result of your intrepidity and gratefully remember the success which I hope will attend you. By the way, bring me two extra horses, with sabres and carbines. Sergeant Atherton of Stedman's company, who has been studying up infantry tactics every hour he could get off duty, and also posting himself in cavalry drill, will want to go on this expedition. So, also, will Sanders, one of the color-guard, who, I happen to know, has a special liking for Stedman."

The horsemen are mounted, Clinton and Atherton at their head. The whispered injunction of " Watchfulness, silence—forward " is repeated from man to man as Clinton and Atherton, pressing warmly the hand of Harrison, touch their steeds gently, and the detachment is soon out of sight. The colonel, seeking the chaplain's tent asks, "What say you chaplain—what betides?"

"They'll bring them back! "

" Ah, that's a beautiful philosophy of yours, and there's something in it!"

Eager to be first, Atherton and Sanders were permitted

by Clinton to keep in advance and get quite a distance
ahead of their comrades. When a few miles out, they saw,
running toward them, a man, carrying a sabre and pursued
by bloodhounds. It was Stedman, who had broken from
his captors, and Atherton, halting his steed on seeing that
the newcomer was his friend, dealt the foremost of the in-
furiated dogs a sabre blow that dropped him dead as he
was springing on the panting man, a second blow cleaving,
mid-air, the other brute. The other rescuers now came up,
and, leaving a part of his command to protect Stedman,
Lieutenant Clinton, with a dozen of his riders dashed off
after some horsemen who, their advance guard of dogs
having been dispatched, turned southward. They were
soon overtaken, and asked that Clinton allow them to go
back still farther and bury their dead. "Who killed
them?" queried the officer, as, nearing the place where the
"butternuts" lay, he directed two of his men to assist in
the burial.

"Why, that yer mighty peart ain' powerful captain o'
yourn ! We had him tied with cawds, ain' left one o' our
party watchun', while we took a bit o' sleep. Ain' when
the guard got kain o' drowsy, I'll be dog-goned ef that yer
captain did'nt wriggle his hands outen the cawds, ain' afore
we knowed it he prodded that sleepy verdette with the fellow's own sabre, givun' him er stab that put him beyon'
wakun'. How he did the final business fer two more afore
the rest on us knowed it, I'll be dog-goned if I cain tell ye,
but there they be. As I was waked by the hounds that were

hitched out yon', thet captain was gettun' over the bridge yon, that way, ain' up the road by the crick."

"Where are the men captured with Stedman?"

"Up ter Pinckney's camp. 'Pears like 'twas the cap'n he most wanted ter git inter prison."

As Clinton and Atherton, at the head of the rescuing party, neared the path diverging that led to their own camp at the right, Atherton said:—

"Listen! far to the left I hear—Crack! crack,! bang, bang, bang! yes, pickets driven in, and—r–b–r, r–b–r, r–b–r, r–b–r, r–b–r, t–r, t–r, t–r—yes, the long roll sounds at the rebel camp. I wonder if Colonel Harrison has made a night march to capture Pinckney? Yes, hear the firing? There! the rebel yell!

The Clinton detachment found but two companies of in-fantry in camp; and the rest of the cavalrymen were also gone. Explanation of the absence came an hour later, when Major Tompkins and his horsemen appeared, fol-lowed by three hundred sorry looking "gray backs," behind whom marched the eight companies of the Thirteenth, Colonel Harrison in command, and the foremost company carrying their pieces with fixed bayonets. The South-erners were placed under a double guard, preparatory to a compelled journey to imprisonment, "In the land o' Yankee Doodle," as Bill Jones remarked in answer to a query of one of the captured. When Clinton's captives were placed with the others, one of them asked of an ac-quaintance, "Where is Colonel Pinckney?"

"Why, yer see, he got right smart cross over a lot o'
apple-jack, jes' afore the Yanks come, ain' he know'd no
more wisdom nor a chickun. Ain' I'll be dog-goned ef he
didn't hold his shooter up ter the face of Harrison, the
leader o' them yer Yanks, ain' I recon' more'n a dozen
rifles o' their'n was leveled straight at Pinckney's head
right smart quick. Ain' he died of an overdose o' Yankee
pills! He's tucked inter the sain' with thirty more o'
we uns. Ain' I don't care ef Pinckney did get knocked
over, he's so dog-goned, pizen mean. Why, when one of
them yer Tennessee fellers that was 'scripted inter our
regiment telled another on em that 'twas rough fer Pinckney ter insult Stedman, Pinckney, th' ole cuss, hearn on't,
ain' hed that yer mountaineer strunged up by the thumbs,
where he was a-hangun' when the Yanks come. Ain' when
Harrison seed thet feller a-danglun' he cut them air cawds
right smart quick!"

At the next parade of the Thirteenth, an order from
Colonel Harrison was read by Adjutant Jameson, thanking
the infantry and cavalry for their exploits, and making
special mention of Stedman, Clinton, Sanders, and the
"ever timely man, on whose heeding of his intuitions,
turned all the successes that made a night bright with
bravery, that would have been dark without the opportune
acts of the pious and patriotic Chaplain John Peters."
And the order continued :—

"The colonel commanding regrets to announce the
death of ten brave men, who were foremost in the attack

on the camp of the enemy, one of whom, the first sergeant of company A, was the first man to scale the breastworks. The vacancy caused by this death is filled by the pro-motion of Sergeant Edward Atherton, whose bravery against hounds and man in the rescue of Captain Stedman, entitles him to the gratitude of his comrades and his com-mander."

"Mother," said Agnes Smith, as she came from a call at the house of the Dawsons, where she had read, from a letter of Frank to his father, an account of the events of the memorable night, "mother, you knew better than I! Mother, I thank you for what you said to me. Isn't—isn't Edward brave!"

"Yes, Agnes, I understand. God bless you, my dear. And let us never cease to pray for the protection of Heaven on our loved ones."

CHAPTER VII.

CERTAIN DOCUMENTS.

OFTEN was the vision of the prayerful Peters taken by Colonel Harrison to guide him in his campaigning, and always with success to prove the wisdom of the heeding, he gaining by it victories which, without it, he could not have achieved, and avoiding dangers which otherwise would have come upon his command. And in 1863, there was a "leading," obedience to which was to bring its followers to success in civil affairs.

"Colonel Harrison," said Peters, as he entered headquarters, of a June morning, "I want to say a word."

"All right, chaplain, what is it?"

"War is attended with casualties and none of us know who may fall first. I've often thought of those Atherton inventions, the returns for which there is no doubt that Lemuel Barnes has, through fraud, been receiving all these years. Sergeant Jones, I believe, knows something which, if duly given in a sworn statement might be of value, and perhaps, pivotal, in a suit brought in behalf of the son of the inventor, against Barnes, to recover pay for that which he has wrongfully taken. It now seems to me wise to do something in the matter."

"Chaplain, I have found your intuitions come true so many times that I shall act on this suggestion. You remember that I was justice of the peace up at Wayfield, and perhaps an oath taken before me here would be regarded in the courts.   Please call Sergeant Jones, and, he willing, as I presume he will be, the deposition shall be taken and forwarded, if you please, to Mrs. Harrison for safe keeping, until we get out of the business now on our hands, a duplicate of the same to be made out and sent to Mrs. Jameson, to guard."

And in due form the documents aforesaid were sent north by the next mail to leave camp.

The day before Mrs. Jameson received the duplicate, she was driving with her father Esquire Belmont and her child, and noticed in the road, soon after meeting Lemuel Barnes, who was going to Ridgeway, a large envelope which proved to be unsealed, and from which the paper it contained had slipped partly out, revealing the words, "Edward Atherton's assignment of patents to Lemuel Barnes, 1848 and 1850."   The handwriting Esquire Belmont recognized as that of Mr. Barnes, and opening the paper, he examined the name that purported to be the autograph of the assignor, and remarked, "Marion, that signature was written by Lemuel Barnes!   Mrs. Taylor has informed me that she has a drawing made by Mr. Atherton, on which there's a specimen of his handwriting. Of course we have no right to retain this document.   But I propose to hold it long enough to have Mr. Evartson compare the signature with the handwriting on the paper which Mrs. Taylor has, and to have a picture of the autographs on the so-called assignment taken by the photographer who has located in our village, and who, as I have learned, is one who can be trusted." Suiting action to words, Belmont, two hours later, returned the paper unharmed to the envelope, which was superscribed with Barnes's address in his own handwriting, and sealing and stamping it, deposited it at the post office, whence it was taken that evening, by the owner on his return from Ridgeway.

Going home, he treated Mrs. Barnes to this characteristic fault-finding, which she, in the accustomed meekness and patience with which she endured the arrogant and censorious man, received with no other response than a sigh :—

"I wish you'd be more careful about fixin' up my pockets, so's't I sha'n't be loosin' money and important documents. It's a pretty pass things have come to if you can't spend time ter take a few stitches an' so save your beloved husband from dropping papers that's worth as much as a farm. The Scripture commands us ter be diligent in business, which means, as our beloved Brother Barber said, in his sermon, Sunday morning, 'faithful in all things committed to us.'"

And the next day Lemuel Barnes was "diligent in business," going to the post-office promptly on the arrival of the mail in which he expected his monthly remittance for the use of the Atherton inventions, and taking, from one of the letters he received, drafts to the amount of fifteen hundred dollars, which he placed in his safe, to be deposited to his credit at the Wayfield bank, the day following. Remarking to his "beloved wife" that he must call on Brother Barber, to confer concerning "the interests of Zion," Deacon Barnes went to the parsonage, where he met "Squintus" Beals, the other deacon, and Jeremiah Joslyn. "The interests of Zion" having been discussed by the quartette of "fore-ordained and elected," and the "backslidings of Israel" having been appropriately bemoaned by the "weeping prophet," prayer was offered by "Brother Barber" for the "watering of the waste places of Zion," and thereafter "Squintus" and Joslyn departed, the redoubtable chief of the "fore-ordained and elected" remaining for the supplementary act of paying Barber his quarterly installment of salary, to which was added the bonus of twenty dollars as Barnes's personal recognition of the value of the services of the "most excellent pawstor in all these parts," a remembrance that elicited from the minister a promise to "pray that the good Lord continue to be gracious to our Zion, and to bless those who stay up the hands of His servant!"

CHAPTER VIII.

AT GETTYSBURG.

DECIMATED in battle and wasted by disease, the Thirteenth received, to replenish its ranks, four hundred men from the region whence came those who had fallen. Ridgeway sent fifty manly fellows; there were a hundred and more from Wayfield; a few came from Hardland, and among those that Dayville sent was Fred Sloan, son of the farmer on the Hardland road, at whose place Elder Peters was wont to exchange horses when on his rounds as an itinerant in the ante-bellum days. Another is Mike Tobin, who, as "the childther" have grown older, has at last, obtained the consent of his Gretchen to "join the sojers an' fight with Bill Joanes, against the ribils," and who is delighted to find his request granted to be assigned to fill a vacancy in the color-guard beside his old friend.

The Army of the Potomac is at Gettysburg! And of all the thousands of that war-worn host none braver than the Thirteenth! The legions gaze across the lovely valley of fertile farms covered with the blossomed wheat and bordered on either hand by eminences whose grassy slopes remind them of the hillside pastures in New England, whereon fed the herds of their fathers, and of homes there, endeared to them by the associations of boyhood! With the emotions of awe and delight inspired by the grandeur and beauty of the scene, they mingle feelings of patriotism, and they nerve themselves to the determination to behave bravely in the conflict with the on-coming foemen. And their apprehension tells them it is to be more terrible than any contest of their previous campaigns! Officers of the line and members of the staff are self-sustained and thoughtful. Harrison, mounted, scans the regiment, his eyes running along the whole front; and, leaning in his saddle, he grasps the hand of his adjutant and says: "Jameson, every man of the Thirteenth is a hero!"

"Yes, colonel, you are right, and they have a cool and courageous commander," quietly responded Jameson.

"Who is well supplemented with the wisdom of his adjutant," replied the leader.

The chaplain who has come to be regarded not only as protecting angel of the regiment, but as prophet of its destinies, as well, is the picture of prayerful anxiety. Yet on his face hope is dawning above the doubts. He reins his horse near Captain Cushman, speaks in an undertone and presses warmly the hand of his comrade. Halting near Captain Sherwood, he takes the extended hand, and says, the very soul of the man speaking in his tones, "Sherwood, may the God of battles protect us to-day, and give victory to the flag of the Thirteenth and of the country!" With greetings to others of the line in passing to the right, he halts by Captain Stedman, saying, "God bless you, captain," and continues, as the first sergeant and others of the right company, for a moment, step from their places to take the hand of their friend, "And God bless you, Atherton, and all the boys from Dayville." Returning, he halts and dismounts near the color-guard, and says, as he takes the hands of Tobin and Jones, "You'll do your duty, and may Heaven protect those who guard the ensign of Liberty!"

The time for action has come, and welcome to his men are the words of Harrison, words which are spoken to be heeded but that are not, and seem not, the dictum of a ruler, but that are, rather, the rallying cry, the inspiring signal utterance of a leader loved for his humanity and admired for his bravery.

"Fire, Thirteenth!"—and at the summons the soldiers shoot with a precision of aim that tells on the ranks of the enemy and teaches him that he wars against skilled marksmen and with a persistency which shows that his opponents have the determination of courageous men and the devotion of patriots. Again the voice of the chief, "That's right, boys, how finely you pepper them and how cool you behave under fire!" So much of a man that he is a good deal of a soldier, Harrison contrasts with Ridgeway, the lieutenant-colonel, who, so much of a martinet that he is nothing of a soldier, thinks that the other pays too little attention to military usage and that even in the emergencies of actual war he ought to employ the routine phraseology of command prescribed in the books of tactics, unvaried by the words of direction originating at the time in his own mind and especially not elivened by the words of cheer springing from his heart, thinks that in those emergencies, for acting in many of which no fit rules could be prescribed in advance, he ought to act in accordance with prescribed rules. In the army, as everywhere else, the stickler for rules and precedents is usually a small man and often a cold man,—not infrequently a heartless one; and, small and cold enough to be wholly incapable of generosity, he is often fevered with jealousy and capable of the intensity of hate. Such an one seems Ridgeway, his face naturally expressionless except for its sternness, speaking the envious heart within that begrudges Harrison the liking that his naturalness calls forth from his men and the devotion that his goodness inspires. And, always thinking him to be such an one, Harrison, wise as he is brave, natural and good, and always looking toward harmony in his command, has managed so that he has not only prevented anything arising to provoke the jealous man to work unpleasant results, difficult as it must have been, but so as to keep him from knowing or suspecting that his superior thought him jealous. And, now, after a few hours of methodically, mechanically, and heartlessly performed duty of supplementing the colonel in directing the work of the regiment, Ridgeway is wounded, and Harrison, leaning in his saddle, whispers to his adjutant :—

"Jameson, the gods be praised! See Johnson alone, and ask him to keep Ridgeway till he gets well!"

"All right, colonel, I understand."

The second day of the conflict begins and calm amid

the tumult moves the leader along the line of his legion, smiling in frequent recognition of the bravery of the soldiers and his voice ever and anon heard in the pauses of the deafning din of the conflict as he cheers his men with, "Nobly done, my braves, nobly done! You'll make the name of the Thirteenth immortal!" or "It's terrible, my heroes, but you're equal to the emergency. The gods will protect you, my noblest of men." Then, after retiring for a few moments for the surgeon to set and dress an arm broken by a rebel bullet, he returns on the gallop, exclaiming, "They're saucy, boys, but I've one hand left. Go in, boys, go in!" And "go in" they do, each man at sight of the commander with an arm in a sling vowing, as more than one whispers to the man beside him, "We'll pay the Johnnies for that!" A regiment of reserves comes down on the run to carry, at this point, the line of the army. Harrison's musical voice is cheerful summons to his men : "A regiment will make our places good here. Vow, each man, to drop a dozen! Forward, double-quick, march!" Then came, "Halt! Fire!" And a half of the assailants fall. Harrison's order, "Fix bayonets!" finds quick heeding. With a recklessness that in a better cause would have been admirable, on come the remainder to perish, most of them, transfixed on the steel that bristles to receive them! A hundred alone remain who, dropping their guns at the demand of Harrison, to surrender, are double-quicked to the rear, under guard, and are soon en route northward.

Another day of the conflict, and how terribly rages the battle! How transformed the scene of loveliness that was! The fields of blooming wheat are beaten and powdered by the tramp of contending battalions and squadrons, ploughed with the carriages of the quaking artillery, and strewn with dead horses and men and all the horrid debris of war! The missiles from the thundering cannon scream above the soldiery with the music of hell and smoke that renders it almost impossible to distinguish friend from foe, rises in clouds that obscure the sun in heaven! But nothing can prevent Harrison's men from seeing him or shut them from his sight. The serried front of the Thirteenth that seems of almost adamantine firmness, suffers fearful decimation from the fire of the foe, but the survivors readily "close up" to fill the vacancies and the war goes on. The quick eye of the leader notes the thinning, and, though saddened by the fall of every one, he is still calm amid the surges of the conflict! By his cheery voice and equipose of bearing inspiring his men to steadiness of behavior in the tide, in every movement giving evidence of strength of mind and courage of heart equal to the terrible ordeal, and by his serenity of mien seeming to challenge the war, he appears to his men something beyond the heroic and invested with the power and the prescience of the skies!

The brigade commander has fallen and Harrison assumes charge of the whole five regiments, deputizing Major Walbridge to the immediate charge of his own regi-

ment, where that officer gives good account of himself
until he falls in leading an attack later in the day, when
the command of the regiment comes to Captain Stedman,
the senior of the line. This officer is soon thrice wounded
and is carried from the field. Then Captain Cushman of
the color company assumes charge only to sound the rallying cry of, " Forward Thirteenth!" when he is shot in the
breast and falls into the arms of Chaplain Peters. Bending to the face of the dying warrior, the minister hears the
whispered words, "Tell Ethel and Teddy good-bye, and
say that I died for the old flag!"

Captain Sherwood is now in command of the regiment.
The lieutenants of Stedman's company have been disabled,
and the command devolves on the first sergeant, who, as
Colonel Harrison still watchful of his own regiment, nears
him and says, " Atherton, I shall depend on you." responds,
"Yes, Colonel Harrison." Then, seeing a full company
of the enemy coming towards the centre of the regiment
as if to capture the colors, he commands, " Company A,
left wheel—halt—fire!" A score of the attacking company
drop dead in their tracks. Before the assailants are near
enough to have the oblique firing from Atherton's men
endanger the comrades of the latter, a second volley
damages the foe more than the first, and the sergeant
commands, "Company A, right, backward, dress—front!
He has reduced the rebel company to thirty, and his men
and all the regiment have close work to repel the attack
now made all along the line. The southrons who are bent

on the centre, advance and ten of them fall from the well
directed aim of the pieces of the color-guard, who, as the
foemen halt to fix bayonets for a charge, dispatch a dozen
more, while several of their own number fall at their side,
leaving five by the colors and eight about to spring like
tigers to sieze them! Three of the grays fall and two of
the guard, leaving Mike Tobin, Sanders with the state ensign, and Bill Jones with the larger flag. Tobin's quick
firing fells two of the five rebels when, seeing the others
aiming their pieces directly at the head of his friend, the
indignant Celt, his eyes aflame and his red locks seeming
to blaze with unwonted heat of color, springs at them with
inverted musket upraised and exclaims, "Bad luck to yez!
hurrting Bill Joanes! bad luck to yez!" emphasizing each
utterance with a blow that brings down its victim. The
last of the assailants gives Jones a fatal bayonet thrust in
his breast, when the bloody and brain-smeared musket of
the irate Irishman descends and the rebel falls, his head
literally broken in pieces by the terrible blow! And Tobin, turning, moans out his grief at the loss of his comrade by whose side he kneels:—

"Bill Joanes, Bill Joanes! me own dacint Bill Joanes!
The frind of Moike Tobin all these yares, an' shure, Bill
Joanes, Bill Joanes!" Then, bending, he whispers, "Can
ye shpake, Bill Joanes?" The eyes of the dying man open
and his faint voice is, "Good-bye, Mike Tobin, good-bye;
Jake Sanders, good-bye!"

Chaplain Peters, who has left others with the form of

Captain Cushman, kneels by the dying standard-bearer and whispers, as he takes his hand to feel the ebbing life :—

"My brave man, what word?"

And the expiring soldier whispers :—

"Tell Mollie that I love her—that I'm going home to wait for her. And tell the boys to keep the old flag flying!"

Assisting in carrying the sergeant to a place of safety, Peters returns as Captain Sherwood falls pierced by a dozen bullets, and as the saint and patriot stoops to lift the lifeless form, he is wounded in one hand, but, heeding not the hurt, bears off his burden.

The death of his comrades places Captain Newton of the Ridgeway company at the head of the torn regiment that went into battle with a thousand and now, as the conflict ceases at sunset, numbers but five hundred! Other regiments of the brigade have suffered like losses, and all of the legions of the union forces leave many a corse on the field of Gettysburg!

Adjutant Jameson, who in addition to his other duties, had kept in his note book, as the rapid work of decimation went on, almost a complete list of the slain and wounded, reported the sad score to his chief on the return of the colonel to the command, at the close of the final day. And he had reported to him the names of many, at the time they fell. On learning of the death of Major Walbridge, the thoughtful man sent a courier from the field to the nearest telegraph station with this message for Reverend Doctor Robinson :—

"Break the news gently to his loved ones—Walbridge is gone!"

When the adjutant rode up and with hushed breath whispered to his leader the names of the Wayfield captains and the standard-bearer, Harrison, sighing, replied, "Jameson, this is terrible, terrible! but their death will intensify the devotion and valor of those who remain." Penciling this message, he handed it to the adjutant, who rode away to despatch it and returned to receive a message for Doctor Robinson containing a list of all the Wayfield men who had fallen :—

"MRS. ANDREW M. HARRISON, WAYFIELD:—
   Tenderly tell the news—Cushman, Sherwood and the brave Bill Jones are gone.   .
                                           A. M. H."

It was the wish of the humane heart of Colonel Harrison, as he surveyed the sad scene after each battle, that it was possible for him to send home for burial the remains of all his band who had perished. But, this being out of the question, he did what he could to secure their decent interment and to mark their resting place. And while suffering throughout the engagement at Gettysburg from the wound received on the first day, he was, at all times more mindful of others than of himself, and looking carefully to the welfare of the wounded for whom Major Johnson and his assistant seemed not only skilled surgeons, but angels of mercy, he also ordered a detail of men to bring from the field the remains of Major Walbridge, Sergeant jones, and Captains Cushman and Sherwood. By his direction they were embalmed and sent northward in charge of Adjutant Jameson, who, though wounded, thought himself able to undertake the journey. Accompanying him were Frank Dawson, Jake Sanders, and Mike Tobin, each of whom were promised, a sergeant's warrant "for bravery at Gettysburg," to be given them on their return. Sanders had been appointed to act color-sergeant on the day his predecessor fell, and Tobin received the thanks of his colonel, an hour after his fine fury on the fellows who "hurrt Bill Joanes!" So absorbed had he been in defending his comrade that he learned not of his own wounds until later in the day when, half in earnest and half in meriment he exclaimed, "Pon me sowl, Jake Sanders, the ribils have been hurrting Moike Tobin, an' they have, thin, Jake Sanders, an' shure!"

CHAPTER IX.

"How Sleep the Brave."

TENDERLY bearing the slain heroes to their native New England, the guard of honor were met at a station twenty miles from their destination by Reverend Doctor Robinson, Mr. Smith, Mr. Dawson, Deacon Sherwood, and others, who draped with striping of red, white and blue, bordered with black, the locomotive of the train and the special car containing the forms of the loved ones. Arrived at Wayfield, the committee and guard were met by a deputation of citizens, who escorted the party with their precious burden to the town hall and there relieved the custodians of their charge, placing in keeping of the trust five of the twenty who responded to the call for men to sentinel the deceased as they lay in state. A committee of ladies accompanied the soldiers to the home of Colonel Harrison, where they were treated to a collation. It was served by Mrs. Harrison herself, assisted by her friend Miss Davis, who, midway of the hour of the feast, received a letter, which she retired to the parlors to peruse. Returning, she handed the missive to Mrs. Harrison seconding the act with placing the finger on her lip, in an "aside" with that lady, which seconding the company did not notice and Mrs. Harrison did not heed. Scanning the note a moment, she surprised her guests with the announcement :—

"Ladies and gentlemen, Colonel Timothy Edgerley has been decorated with stars 'for gallant behavior in three battles and especially for bravery on the second day of Gettysburg!' And, in your presence, ladies and gentlemen, I congratulate my friend and companion on the news which, notwithstanding her injuction to the contrary, I have taken the liberty to divulge!"

When the cheers that followed Mrs. Harrison's speech subsided, Miss Davis replied, her face, that was usually well controlled, blushing scarlet as she spoke :—

"And if the authorities at Washington don't promote Colonel Andrew M. Harrison to wear the stars instead of the eagles, I'll write to Mr. Lincoln, myself, to know the reason why!"

The call of Adjutant Jameson for "three cheers for General Edgerley that is, and General Harrison that is to be," found hearty response.

For two hours the people of Wayfield and vicinity visited the hall to view the dead soldiers. And at sunset the doors were closed by the sentinels; and three of the guard of honor, Sanders remaining at home, were driven in Deacon Sherwood's carriage along the well-remenbered road to Dayville, preceded by a hearse with a casket containing the color-sergeant. And this was drawn by Billy, the horse of Elder Peters who, that his equine companion might be spared the hardships and casualities of army life, had left him behind, to the great dislike and grief of the horse. Many an one gifted, it is supposed, with wisdom

higher than that informing the mind of the quadruped, has
objected to giving up that which, when surrendered, was
followed by a greater good, or the sparing from a hurt
that, but for the surrender, would have been sure to come.
The man of all work from the Smith homestead who drove
Billy on this occasion, said he "seemed to know what it
all meant and to think that friends of his master had come,
before whom he must act his best," while Mike Tobin said
to his Gretchen, at evening :—

. " I dunno if the craythur understhand at all, at all. But
did ye see that fwhin they took out the coff'n from the
herris and opened it on the grane fernense the toon hall,
and nayer the horse, fer Mollie Joanes and her childther
ter see the face of Bill Joanes, the annimil fwhinnied an'
fwhinnied ? Yer see that fwhin Elder Peters started off
in the sthage to hould matin's, as he did sometimes, he
left the horrse fer a wake thigther with Bill Joanes, who,
by fadin' him, brought the horrse ter think a hape o'him."

At one o'clock the next day memorial services, for the
Wayfield slain were held in the ancient church of that
town, whose citizens with delegations from every neighborhood of a wide region, filled and surrounded the meeting-
house. Before the pulpit were deposited the three caskets
festooned with flowers and the national emblems. Attended by sympathizing friends and accompanied, each,
by her fatherless son, the widows of the warriors wept in
pews where crape added its sombre emphasis, while similar
drapings were about the choir gallery, in which Captain

Cushman had so long sung. And, intensifying the significance of the occasion, was the presence of the custodians
of the dead, who were seated in the open of the auditorium near their charge. Though suffering from wounds
they had held out well on the long journey, which they undertook that they might pay the last tribute of soldiers to
fallen comrades.

Eloquent but simple, brief but comprehensive, the prayer
of the poet and preacher, Reverend Wilbur F. Warren, after
which there was a dirge. Then Reverend Doctor Robinson
arose, and, struggling finally to the full control of his
tremulous voice, said, with the emphasis of calmness indicating the strength which, in one voicing great sorrow,
is welcome and inspiring to the mourning hearts for whom
he speaks :—

"FELLOW COUNTRYMEN :—

A patriotic people mourn their braves and the theme trandscends
the power of human speech! For who can pronounce with fitting
reverence for their worth, admiration for their bravery, love for their
patriotism, and regard for those bereaved by their taking off, the
names of the heroic Walbridge, and Sherwood, and Cushman, and
William Jones the standard-bearer, and others of like fervency of devotion and persistency of courage who fought beside them at Gettysburg, and with them fell on that ensanguined field! Or, who can
speak thoughtfully enough the names of those of ours whose valor
was attested in others of the battles of this most terrible war that
reddens the pages of history!

With muffled drums, and drooping flags, and arms reversed, and
bowed heads, and measured tread, we come bringing to this church of
the fathers, the caskets containing the forms of our heroes, which
when these poor words are said and the requiem sung, we shall bear
to their final rest by the graves of their ancestors.

Grateful for the faith which prompts the prediction that the people will be quick to learn, and glad to heed, the lessons of patriotism which these sacrifices so plainly and eloquently teach, and will prize the liberties for the reëstablishing and perpetuating of which they are made, I cannot think that they will need to be asked to give, in readiness of abundance, the choicest of their sympathy to those bereaved by the loss of the manly ones, whom they held dear as life itself. But what human compassion can suffice? For they are overwhelmed with a sorrow that exceeds all commiseration of men and that can be endured only with the aid of the Divine Benignity! O, Thou pitying Christ,

'Strong Son of God, Immortal Love!

'Thou man of sorrows and acquainted with grief,'

'Jesus lover of their souls,
Let them to Thy bosom fly!'"

An event like this that calls us here, not only teaches the duty of sympathizing with those who mourn, but shows to us how beautiful compassion is, and, how high a privilege he has who is called to be compassionate! And still other good may result from the great calamity. For so great afflictions shame and banish the exclusiveness and selfishness of the sorrow of common griefs; while still further influencing us to unselfishness is the fact that our loss is but one of the many that have come to the people of the land. Citizens of Wayfield, we weep, and our tears mingle with those of the bereaved in every town and hamlet of our beloved New England! And so, all over the loyal states are darkened homes where bleeding hearts mourn for those who fell with our heroes at Gettysburg, or Donelson, or Roanoke Island, or Port Hudson, or Vicksburg, or on deck of the man of war, or for those who have endured, as have some of our own Thirteenth, the most terrible of all the fates of war, and perished amid the horrors of Andersonville! While to the caves and mountain fastnesses of their region have fled the Unionists of Eastern Tennessee, from those who have persecuted them almost to death, for their love for the flag. Ah, this fraternity of grief of the war for the Union! By what baptism of sorrow have the membership been initiated! Aye, mourning myriads, wherever ye weep, 'we are one with you now!' And with you we cry out in the midst of our sorrow, O, Lord, how long? Yet while saddened with you at thought of the great cost in human life which has been paid, and must continue to be paid, in the cause of good government and the freedom of a race, we accept with you the ordeal of sacrifice the people are called to make on the altar of the country!

> ' O, God, our help in ages past,
> Our hope for years to come,'

we implore Thy benediction on these, and on all, who mourn the loss of loved ones slain. And we look to Thee to give continued wisdom and courage to our great leader, the matchless Lincoln! Inspire our soldiers to new deeds of valor, give success to their arms and grant the country a happy issue from the most terrible emergency in the history of nations!"

When the choir had fitly supplemented the address, the fallen warriors were borne from the place of memorial to the ancient cemetery, where, following the volley by the guard of honor, and tender, and pathetic, and reverent words of benediction by Mr. Warren, the committee designated at a meeting of the ladies of Wayfield, at the head of which were Agnes Smith and Mrs. Jameson, bestowed on the graves the beautiful and abundant floral wreaths, crosses and clusters that spoke the hearts of the sorrowing people.

Following the occasion at Wayfield, came the ceremonies over the color-bearer at Dayville, where his neighbors and acquaintances filled the chapel of the New Lights to overflowing, and a thousand more from the vicinity thronged the grounds and stood in respectful silence during the obsequies. The Smiths and Taylors wept in sympathetic nearness to the soldier's widow and son, whose pew was

draped with the emblems of mourning, while near by the
pulpit the encoffined form of the brave one was covered
with roses, and the stars and stripes were festooned on the
pulpit front.   Fatigued with the previous duties of the
day, two of the guard were compelled to forego the sad
pleasure of participating in the ceremonies that remained,
but Adjutant Jameson and Sergeant Tobin conquered the
feebleness caused by their wounds and the long journey
from the seat of war, and appeared in charge of their
fallen comrade.

A fine rhythmic tribute of the gifted Warren to "The
guardians of the flag," was sung by Mrs. Jameson with
melting and tuneful tenderness of voice; and Doctor Robinson spoke the high popular regard for the departed, "for
the man that he had always been and the nobler man developed in becoming the good soldier that he was," and
told the "interest of the people in the cause for which he
warred and died."   Covered with a copy of the colors
that he had defended, and followed by a great concourse
of people, the form of the standard-bearer was borne to
Hillside Rest, that had been hallowed by the burial of
three other soldiers who fell earlier in the war.   And
Agnes Smith laid a wreath of roses on each of the graves,
and, remarked to Mrs. Jameson, and others, who accompanied her to assist in the bestowment, "Would'n't it be
a good thing to repeat this act!"

"It would, indeed," responded Mrs. Jameson, "the oftener
the better; and it ought to be done at least once a year."

And, the child who began at Dayville, the beautiful custom of adorning the sanctuary with flowers, originated at
Wayfield and Dayville, years later, the ceremony of deco-
rating the resting places of the soldier dead with flowers,
that has since become the stated annual observance of
the American people, in remembering those who died for
the Union.

The rays of the setting sun welcoming the standard-
bearer to his rest, glinted among the foliage of the trees
that above his grave swayed with the sighing zephyrs and
seemed to say, "We accept as sad but high honor the
trust of sentineling the repose of dust so sacred as his,
who bravely guarded and firmly upheld the colors of the
Thirteenth and of his country!" The volley from the
muskets of his comrades, not more spoke their farewell
to him, than the signal for renewal of attack on the
enemy's lines; while the sunset, in the dawn that it prophe-
sied, augured victory for the Union armies, and peace for
the country, and symbolized the reward of patriotism to
which the spirit of the brave and true man had been called
in the land of the blest!

Daniel Smith, as he drove home from the burial, said to
the one with him, "Elizabeth—those flowers, years ago—
the beautiful disposition and fine womanliness of that
Agnes of ours—this growing town, and how much more
Heaven only knows! And all resulting, under Providence,
from the act of giving up my selfish will and allowing you
to purchase the flowers. And, now, this sad but beautiful

significance added to the other bright results of that act. For some of the flowers on the grave of the color-bearer here, and on the places where his comrades were laid at Wayfield, grew where, then, those flowers grew—ah, Elizabeth!"

"Yes, dearest, and with the roses bestowed, were marigolds and sweet-williams, that are lineal descendants of those that grew from the seeds bought with the piece of money you gave me then. I have gathered the seeds each year and I know whereof I speak. And, my own, I thank you for the frankness of your acknowledgment. It is worth more than gold to me."

"O, how unspeakable the joy resulting from that self-conquering! Father in heaven, I thank Thee, I thank Thee! for Thou didst help me then to do that act which was the beginning of all my joy!"

A beautiful incident of the occasion at the Wayfield church, came like a gleam of sunshine to brighten the gloomy scene. As the widows of the slain warriors were sobbing around the coffined forms of the heroes and an indescribable intensity of sympathy held the audience in breathless stillness, Teddy Cushman, looking up to his mother, to whose hand he was clinging, said, "Mamma, I'll be good to you; it won't be long before I grow up, and then I can take care of you!"

"Brave one," said Doctor Robinson, who overheard the remark and took the lad to his heart, continuing, "God bless you my boy!" A letter of the minister to Chaplain

Peters noted the incident, which coming to the knowledge of the regiment, the boy was elected "son of the Thirteenth," and new vows were made to battle all the more for the loss sustained by the death of his father. Captain Cushman's company, to the command of which, by the way, Lieutenant Morley had been promoted, made up a purse for Teddy which was forwarded to Mrs. Harrison by the colonel, with instructions to place it, with as much more from himself, at interest for the child.

When Doctor Robinson called at evening to condole with Mr. Sherwood, the bereaved man, raising his bowed head, said, with a calmness of tone to which he had brought his husky voice :—

"It is, indeed, a great price to pay, this wealth of treasure and of blood; but it is a glorious cause in which the offering is made! And, my friend, shots like those fired to-day over the resting places of our loved ones, speak not only the grief of many loyal hearts but the death-knell of the rebellion, or a sure prophecy of that end. And, the sun in his strength shining on all the country and with plenteous rains causing the fields of the North to yield abundant harvests to feed those who toil at home, and those who war at the front, is, in its majesty of beneficence, emblematic of the peace and prosperity which, with the success that is sure to come to the armies of the Union, shall dawn bright over all the land!"

CHAPTER X.

PEACE AND WAR.

OF a morning of August, 1863, gazing southward from
the veranda of the "Sunnyside" cottage of the
thriving settlement of Friends near the Pennsylvania town of Cohecton, is one whose raven locks contrast pleasantly with her white robing and with the glow
of health on the features that vies with the rose breathing
perfume from a bosom thrilling with expectancy, but calm
with assurance that some joy long wished for is soon to
be realized. Yet enough of query is evident in manner
and mien to excite interest and prompt a conclusion that
she does not know how soon the realization will come
and has an occasional fear that some fatality may rob her
of that joy. And the color of health and the hope beaming in the eye hide not the fact that wearing anxiety has
left its sobering traces on the lineaments of a face that
speaks of love, loyalty, constancy, and — womanliness.
Rereading for the dozenth time a letter which she informs
a Quakeress sitting by her side, "is the last he wrote before Gettysburg," she tucks it carefully in a package of
missives that are all superscribed in the same bold hand,
and, scanning several telegrams, places them by the package and resumes the southward gaze across the landscape,
over which it is evident her vision has swept until every
detail is familiar.

Ezekiel Slayton has just returned from Cohecton to Sunnyside and as he enters the carriage-way, he halts at the end of the veranda and says :—

"Lillie, thee looks anxious, but I think thee need have no doubt." Handing his daughter a Philadelphia paper, the Quaker drives back the carriage-way.

"Will you read for me?" asks the one in white.

And the woman in drab responds with a column account of developments "at the front," and says, "Lillie, I think thee has not long to wait. May I read the words which the telegraph boy brought?" And Miss Slayton read:

"Thank Heaven! he is beyond danger. The bullet is extracted, the sabre wound is doing well, and so is the broken arm.

LUKE JOHNSON, M. D.,
Major and Surgeon 13th Regiment."

Other telegrams indicated continued improvement, and the last read, "He has started." And Miss Ten Eyck, said, "He may come this evening."

"Perhaps this afternoon, but there is nothing certain in war time."

Hannah Slayton did not notice the mingled look of joy and mischief on her father's face as he came home. He had not told her of meeting some one who wished his coming unannounced.

"If that isn't!"—and, while from the carriage-way, where he had come, Ezekiel Slayton, unsurprised, beheld the enactment from beginning to culmination, Lillie Ten Eyck flew down the walk, out the gate and along the roadside,

and was soon hidden under the cloak hanging from the
shoulders of a stalwart soldier, who, grasping her with his
right arm, bestowed a kiss which met a response that
was such an invitation to renewal of· attack as the brave
Captain Thomas Stedman could not decline.

From their gaze into the brown eyes above her, eyes of
liquid blue turn satisfied.   Then they look with tenderness
on the left arm in the sling; and, disengaging herself from
the embrace, Lillie unbuckles the sword from her warrior
lover and taking up the blanket-roll which he had dropped
at the meeting, and readily catching his step—for what
woman cannot keep step with the man she loves !—she
walks by his side, carrying blade and baggage, to the veranda; and, dropping her load, she introduces :—

"Captain Stedman—my friend Hannah Slayton,—you
remember her."   And the Quakeress, as she leads the
soldier to a seat, and lifts his hand to her lips, responds :—

" It was good of thee and others like thee to try to stop
the bad war.   Thy friend Lillie told me thee was much
hurt in the fighting.   But I hope thee will get well.   Thee
is welcome to Sunnyside.   With thy war clothes thee does
not look like our people.   But he that defends his country
is a friend to the Friends !   Thee come, if thee please, to
the keeping room.   Father and I are to dine at Aunt
Hannah's house this afternoon, and thy friend Lillie might
like to see thee more here.   Aunt will want to see thee,
for thy friend Elizabeth Smith of New England, who once
lived with her, and who, as aunt remembers had a discern-

ing mind, wrote good things of thee. And we all hope
thee will get strong before thee goes back to the war place.
Thee please excuse me now?"

"Charming, delightful," said Stedman to his friend,
"that sincerity and directness, that innocence and wisdom
—Lillie, I congratulate you on having such a home. What
a contrast to the place where I first saw you. Thank
heaven, Lillie, for that meeting! How your letters have
cheered me! And how glad I am to see you so well and
to find you in this paradise of peace and quiet that contrasts so beautifully with the din and carnage of war!
Lillie!"—and the strong arm that had smitten down his
country's foes lifted her to his knee, and tenderly but earnestly he gave a kiss and lingered at her lips to drink the
bliss of an accepted lover, who needed not the words that
came—"In answer to the question of your last letter—
Thomas Stedman, all yours, and forever!"

"Mine! Mine!!"

An hour later a gentle rap at the door was answered by
Miss Ten Eyck, and the Quakeress introduced two of her
friends who had called, and in an aside with Stedman's
friend she suggested that he be shown the best chamber.

An hour of completest rest in that upper room of the
home of the disciples of peace, and the wounded warrior
from Gettysburg, at the summons of a gentle rap and a
gentler voice, "Thee wish dinner now?" descended to the
repast in waiting. Plain indeed were the viands of the
board, but prepared with that perfection of the culinary

art which your accomplished Quakeress so well under-
stands. And had there been but a dry crust, instead of
the fresh pulpy biscuit and peaches and cream, that, for
sweetness and richness, put to shame the nectar of the
gods, the feast would still have been royal, when at the
table was Miss Lillie Ten Eyck, who, in the eyes of the
gallant warrior, seemed, in the perfection and beauty of
her young womanhood, almost divine! When came the
sunset to mellow the scene at the Sunnyside cottage of
Cohecton, at the asking of Luke Gray, a Quaker physician,
who, with his sister Ruth, was guest of the Slaytons,
the soldier began an account of the great battle of
the war.

In the midst of the narrative he was interrupted by the
arrival of the evening mail, that included a heavy envelope
superscribed, "Major Thomas Stedman, Care of Mr.
Ezekiel Slayton, Cohecton, Pa.," receiving which he exclaimed, " Queer title they give me, and its in Harrison's
handwriting, too !"

Opening the letter Stedman said, "There! that's the
meaning of the meeting of officers which they held while
I was in the hospital and about which they kept so dark!
It's one of Colonel Harrison's 'flank movements.' I'll
get even with the noble fellow, yet."

Handing the paper to Miss Ten Eyck, Stedman continued , "The letter means, ladies and gentlemen, that un-
known to me the officers of the Thirteenth, at the asking
of Colonel Harrison, have chosen me, and the governor

of our state has commissioned me, in the place of the late Major John Walbridge."

" And," added Miss Ten Eyck, "it reads 'for gallant behavior before the enemy at Gettysburg.' "

A telegram extended Stedman's furlough, and a letter said Harrison was going home and that the former on his return·would command the regiment during the absence of the latter, Lieutenant-Colonel Ridgeway to be given a furlough when Stedman came back.

At a Philadelphia passenger station a tall soldier had bidden two ladies good-bye, and had stepped from the waiting-room, when he heard his name spoken from the open car window of a train en route to Washington and the front. Looking up he exclaimed, "Why, Harrison!" Jumping toward the extended hand, he pressed it with a soldier's heartiness, and, going to the waiting-room, he escorted the ladies to the train, and introduced—"Colonel Harrison—Miss Slayton ; Miss Ten Eyck."

The train began to move, and, seizing his luggage, he stepped on a car platform, and lifting his hat to those from whom he had parted, entered the coach, saying, " Harrison, why so soon returned? I am going back on time, am I not?

" A day ahead—just like you; and, to explain—when seeking a furlough I had an intuition that 'would not down' that something wrong might happen to Sergeant Atherton, whom Captain Grout, as you know, dislikes. But, as the

regiment, for its behavior, had been given a respite from
active work, I thought it the best time I should have to
see my wife from whom I had been absent two years, and
my boy whom I had never seen. So, when I had made a
surprise on you,"—"Just like you," interjected Stedman—
"I started, leaving the faithful Chaplain Peters to watch,
and telegraph me in cipher, at New York, if Grout or that
martinet Ridgeway, attempted any abuse of Atherton.
Mrs. Harrison was to meet me at the office of Lewis
Darling, whom you will remember as a school-teacher in
New England, and who is now a merchant and manufact-
urer at New York. She arrived just after I did, and we
were ten minutes together, when a messenger brought a
dispatch for me to come at once. What was I to do?
Adjutant Jameson was ill, and if well, he was subject to
the commander of the regiment; the surgeon was on duty
at the general hospital, and if by telegraphing you I had
found you well enough for duty and sent you to assume
command, leaving Ridgeway to go home, that would have
delayed a day, which might have been as long as forever.
There was my wife from whom I had been separated two
years, that seemed eternities! And there was my own son
and namesake on whom I had never looked until then,
and who, having been schooled by his mother, had so
acquainted himself with my features as he saw them in a
portrait at home that, on seeing me with my officer's coat
displaced by a citizen's coat handed me by Mr. Darling,
exclaimed, "Papa!" Tears of joy coursed down my face

at the word! Struggling with emotions far beyond the
power of speech, I asked, 'What shall I do Mary?' when
the heroic woman said with the calmness of earnestness,
'Noblest, mine, although it breaks my heart to say it—go.
And Heaven bless you!' Then pressing her cheek to the
face of the boy in her arms she said to him, 'Kiss Papa,
Andrew!' And the little man, clasping his chubby arms
around my neck as she held him up, gave me a kiss which
was the greatest bliss but one, possible to man on earth,
and that one the kiss that tells him his soul has found its
mate! Mr. Darling, who on my first entering his office,
inquired for Atherton, gave me for him this fine new coat
with the sleeves adorned with the chevrons of a first
sergeant. With another kiss from wife and child I was
soon on my way."

The officers had reached the railway station two miles
from the northern outpost of the army, beyond the cen-
tral camp of which was the Thirteenth; and Chaplain
Peters met them a short distance from the cars. Expect-
ing but one arrival he led but one horse.

"Chaplain, how fare you?—and what is it about Atherton?" said Harrison.

"In brief, of course?"

"The briefest."

"Sergeant Atherton, whom you left in command of his
company, protested firmly but respectfully against the sentence of extra guard duty on two men of that company,

punishment asked by Captain Grout, nominally because
the men appeared at guard-mounting with guns alleged
to be 'so rusty as to be unfit for use,' but which pieces
were really specked but a trifle.   And I doubt not the
sentence was really given to spite Atherton, whose friends
they were—as, in fact, everybody in the regiment who
knows him is a friend of Atherton.   Thinking he had the
right as commander of the company, he made, with increasing urgency of petition, a second and a third request
that the order be revoked.   But Grout was immovable,
and Ridgeway refused to countermand the order, and also,
told Atherton to cease his importuning, which injunction
the sergeant bravely disregarded, and made a fourth request.   Peremptorily refused the petition and threatened
with punishment for a repetition thereof, he replied on the
spot, with dignity of mien, calmness of voice, and a brave
daring of consequences that was sublime :—"

"' Sir, when one asks not a favor, but justice, there's no
rank on earth can give a man the right to say him nay!
This, if the petition is in his behalf who makes it.   Does
he voice the prayer of others for justice, doubly wrong the
refusal.   And, sir, this petition in behalf of my comrades-
in-arms for that which is as just as the sunbeam is lustrous,
I repeat not as a prayer but as a demand, the rightfulness
of which will last "as long as the river runs," or "the
ever during brass" is firm !'   Then a drum-head court-martial—Atherton reduced to the ranks—and at this time, with
a log of wood tied to his shoulders, he, with those whom

he befriended, is pacing at the camp entrance under guard !"

" That best man of the Thirteenth punished ! The boy for whose protection I am commissioned by humanity, by justice, and by the best woman on earth ! he, Edward Atherton, humiliated by David Grout ! Outrageous, fiendish ! damnable ! ! "

" I have brought you the fleetest steed to be found' at the cavalry supply station, to take the place of the horse that was shot under you at Gettysburg.",

" Please allow Stedman, who is yet weak from his wounds, to ride your horse and carry my luggage and his. That will give you a long walk, chaplain."

" All right."

" Let me see" said Harrison, " What shall I christen him ? Ah, I have it." And the warrior sprang to the saddle and, patting his courser's neck, whispered, " Go, Wild-Wind, go ! "

The charger flies past sentinel after sentinel, and camp after camp, and the rider soon catches a glimpse of the colors above the place of his loved band. A few more plunges and the horse halts inside the camp, ploughing his hoofs deep in the earth to quench the fury of his coming.

Harrison, throwing the reins of the foaming steed to the hostler, saying, " Take good care of Wild-Wind, Pomp," hears not the " Yis, sah, Massa Kunnel, Pomp spec you come back on dis yer hoss, when de chapling tuk him."

Springing to the place where Grout's victim was pacing, and saying, as he came up behind him, "Atherton it is your own friend Harrison," the officer cut the cords that bound the log to the sufferer's back. Then, that, overcome as the man was, with gratitude and joy at the sudden rescue, he fall not, the colonel took the soldier's arm, and, chief of the legion though he was, walked with him to headquarters and there, after he had rested for a time on the commander's couch, bade him displace his chevronless coat with one "decorated," as Harrison said, "according to the rank from which you have been reduced and to which you shall be restored, a coat which comes as a present from your old friend and school-master, whom I met in New York."

"God, bless you, Colonel Harrison!"

Major Stedman had arrived, and Atherton, wearing again the insignia of which he had been robbed, went to his tent, where half his company had gathered to congratulate him, and where, when the others had gone, Frank Dawson said, "I've written to your friend, Miss Smith, about this, and you bet I've made a 'few feeble remarks' about that cussed Grout!"

One after another of the officers who voted, at the hastily summoned court-martial, for the findings against Atherton asked by Grout, called on Colonel Harrison to explain and regret their action; and when Grout and Ridgeway, who had not learned of the recanting, appeared to remonstrate with Harrison for his "unmilitary proceeding," he said, addressing Grout, who had used those words of criticism in his complaint:—

"Sir, tyrannizing over one of rank inferior to that which you have held and disgraced, you come to your superior and impudently pronounce on his behavior, characterizing it as 'unmilitary.' I'll not hear you further. Appeal if you choose."

At parade that afternoon Edward Atherton reported, first of the first sergeants—"Company A, all present or accounted for." And there was not a dry eye in all the command—Grout and Ridgeway had concluded to remain in their tents. Cheers burst from the whole line as the adjutant read an order directing that all account of the proceedings against Atherton be "expunged from the records," and the applause was supplemented with "Hail to the Chief," by the musicians, for whom the whole regiment was chorus.

The men of Atherton's company punished with him were exonerated, and they were given a month of freedom from duty, and a clear name on the regimental records.

Ridgeway and Grout remonstrated at brigade head-quaters, where, by the stickler for regulation ways of doing things who was then in command, a hearing was appointed for a week later. He was transferred to another brigade three days after, and when complainants and respondent, with the witnesses re-appeared for the hearing, they were greeted by a very tall officer, whose undress garb gave no index of rank, but whom Colonel Harrison at once recog-

nized and to whose cheery, "Good morning, gentlemen,"
he replied as he grasped the extended hand, "Is this you,
Edgerley?—I'm right glad to see you."

"It is, Colonel Harrison. And, seeing they've given me
stars to wear, I'll show my visitors proper respect by don-
ning a coat with stellar decorations."

When he had heard the case, General Edgerley said:—

"It is urged that the action of Colonel Harrison was
unmilitary, which allegation the evidence adduced does
not warrant. And, if the behavior of the colonel was 'unmilitary,' it was not unmanly; and, with me, always, manliness before military correctness. The case is dismissed."

Grout remonstrated and coupled with his dissent a reference to the time when his superior "was nothin' but a
farm hand, workin' aout fur a livin'." Wholly ignoring
the disrespect of the remark, Edgerley calmly replied:—

"Sir, seeing you have gone into reminiscences, I will
say that the case now decided shows that you have carried
into army life grudges that you once held against the boy
who was then your ward, and will remind you of what I
once before told you; for, Captain Grout, I pity one with
your disposition; yes, I do."

Ridgeway's martinet notions and acts made him so un-
popular in the regiment that he resigned, when, of course,
Major Stedman was promoted to the lieutenant-colonelcy.
But Grout disappointed expectations and did not resign.
There was another engagement soon, and Sergeant Ather-
ton's bravery in the battle won him the thanks of General

Edgerley and a first lieutenant's commission from state
headquarters, while Colonel Harrison obtained for him
and Chaplain Peters furloughs of three weeks. Atherton
started northward at once, to await at Washington, the
arrival of the chaplain, who was to depart the next day.
At a meeting of the line officers, an hour after the lieutenant had gone, Harrison surprised them with the announcement that he had written out his resignation to forward to
state headquarters. He had been thrice tendered a pro-
motion but "a principal reason for resigning," said he, "is
to create a vacancy that I hope will be filled by commis-
sioning Edward Atherton. This suggestion I make at the
request of an officer of the line, and of the lieutenant-
colonel." His associates, who greatly regretted losing
Harrison, voted a series of the most expressive resolutions
of respect and affection ; and, novel though seemed the
idea of promoting a lieutenant over his superiors, to the
command of a regiment, they voted it unanimously. This
result, with Colonel Harrison's resignation, he sent to the
governor by Chaplain Peters, who, journeying with Atherton, from Washington several hours, took a train of a diverging route, saying, as he bade his comrade good-bye,
that he wished to "see a friend at the capital of the
state,"—a truthful remark that did not tell the whole truth.

CHAPTER XI.

A HEAVENLY RECOGNITION:

AN interesting conversation at the home of the Smiths had reached a passage where Miss Agnes, evidently in reply to a very serious question, responded :—

"Yes; I am glad it has come to this; and, Edward Atherton, I am yours forever!"

"Agnes, my own; come!"

Thus much, in the hall, one heard or divined that she heard whispered, one, who, waiting a moment, but not listening, now gave a gentle rap which revealed to her, as it revealed to the lovers, that the door had been left slightly ajar, and who, hearing the voice, "That is you, mother; come," walked leisurely across the parlor to the place sacred to her as the scene of many a petition to Heaven that had brought answers of peace. And there those had risen to greet her to whom her heart went out with affection and hope that spoke from every feature and beamed from her large and loving eyes. To the words, "Mother, Edward and I have pledged," spoken as the two looked trustfully into her face, she responded with a tender kiss for each, following these words of benediction :—

"God bless you, my own, and with you abide a mother's love."

A few moments lingered the three, when, again bestowing a kiss on each, Mrs. Smith said, "Edward, my son, your friend and brother soldier, Chaplain Peters, has come.

He rang half an hour ago at the door admitting to the living room, he must have had an intuition or 'leading,' that, here—well—he has asked to see you, and—Mr. Smith and he are coming through the hall."

With joy beaming on his face, and speaking from his love-lit eye, and giving impetus to his springing step, Edward Atherton, boy once and fatherless, and boy whose soul was motherless and so, who was an orphan worse than orphaned—Edward Atherton, boy once and man now and manly enough to be a boy again, rushed into the arms of his rescuer, teacher, "guide, philospher and friend," and, sobbing in the intensity of his emotion, exclaimed:—

"I thank you, I love you, my dear, dear friend, and ever present angel of blessing! And, O! if, from some celestial height, my sainted father looks down on us, or, if he is near us now in this time of my spiritual exaltation, what emotions of gratitude and of joy are his, as, for the time, he leaves his heavenly employ to witness this earthly scene that is so near, and so like, heaven itself! Hear him as now he speaks; for it is to you:—

'Friend of my son, I thank you, and the Father of us all blesses you, promises you protection in battle, victory for the flag that is the ensign of your band who contend for the right, and before your translation to these abodes of bliss, years in which to proclaim the gospel of Christ with its philosophy of forgiveness of enemies!'

"Hear," continued the raptured man, turning his eyes to Agnes, "for he speaks again :—

'Mate of my son, I send you a father's blessing and the Divine Soul smiles on you and him with ineffable love. And, all ye others who befriended the orphan boy, knów that the Divine Benignity is your friend!'"

Edward Atherton and John Peters had moved from their first position, and the others of the company, in their intensity of interest, had arisen ; and the two were standing on the very spot hallowed by the prayer of their friends, who, now, near them, supported their daughter and waited through moments that seemed to all the group melodious, and perfumed, and restful with the bliss of heaven! The veteran man of God, dear enough and spiritual enough to be welcome even where the souls of lovers held high converse, received on his shoulder the boy, the man, the warrior, the lover! Clasping a hand of Edward Atherton's in both of hers, Agnes Smith was speechless with joy through moments more that seemed to each of them, and to all present, heightened heaven! The lips move and she whispers, "O Father above, I thank Thee! I thank Thee! I pray Thee make me and keep me grateful for the signal honors and unspeakable blessings with which Thou has crowned me in this hour, whose significance shapes my destiny and reaches eternity!"

The door opens gently and a fine manly boy enters and grasps the hand of the minister, who, stooping, kisses him and says, "Wesley, I am right glad to see you. How bright with health and hope your young eyes are."

"Elder Peters, I am glad to see you and glad that those rebels didn't kill you."

"The Lord spared me, my boy," said the minister, and,

turning his gaze full at the young officer before him, he continued :—

"Edward Atherton, when the Highest speaks His benediction, how poor seem the honors of earth! Yet to you, who, with those around us, have heard spoken from heaven words of crowning, comes the message of an earthly ruler, the governor of our state. His missive I bring, saying that you are, by him, commissioned to command a thousand men! Proof of the declaration you will find in this package which is addressed, in the handwriting of His Excellency, to

'Colonel Edward Atherton,
Thirteenth Regiment, Dayville.'"

Mrs. Smith was first to speak, and congratulating Atherton, she continued. "None of us would be selfish in our joys. There are other friends of yours, Edward, who would like to hear of your deserved good fortune."

. "Yes, mother, there are; and I must see them."

As he spoke, the bell rang.

Good Mrs. Taylor had said to her husband, "Samuel. Edward will want to stay there, late, and if we are aged people, let us drive over, to bring him back."

"That's right, Mary,—the dear boy, it does my old heart good to think how well he's done! And that Chaplain Peters, and Stedman, and Colonel Harrison, God bless 'em all!"

And when, kneeling before his foster parents, the boy whom they had given a home in their humble cottage and in their hearts, looked up into their faces and, through blinding tears, read the paper constituting their whilom protegé the leader of a thousand, they were speechless with joy and wonder!

In the "wee, sma' hours" Atherton went to the chamber that had given him repose in the pleasant nights of the years of his boyhood before the war, years that followed the bondage to a tyrant that was worse than war; and the kind woman who bade him good-night at the door said, "Here, Edward, I have, every night, prayed for my boy on the battle-field and for his comrades."

Returning to the living room and opening the Bible, as was the wont of the good woman when joyful or joyless, Mrs. Taylor read the words, "Cast thy bread upon the waters, etc.," and as she turned the leaves she read also, the saying, "He that giveth to the poor lendeth to the Lord."

At the other home, Agnes Smith, as she kissed her mother and father good night, had this thought, "You knew better than I, mother—you predicted well of Edward Atherton."

."Yes, that was my faith, and according to that faith and far exceeding it, is the result."

"Ah, mother, had it not been for you!"

The father, thus—"Yes, Agnes," and pointing to the garden he spoke the one dear name, "Elizabeth!"

"Yes, dearest, I remember."

The salubrious autumn air of the morning that awoke the warrior to the orisons of the first Sabbath of his fur-

lough seemed fresh and perfumed as the breath of June.
With him, along the aisle of the church of the New Lights,
each bearing a floral offering for the pulpit, comes the
girl, now grown to womanly stature and blossoming, who,
in other days, bestowed the homely blooms in the humble
meeting-place of this despised sect that are now fast becoming famous   Uplifted in invocation are the hands of
the saint who then predicted that her act would inaugurate
a custom which would become universal.   The words of
the gifted Warren, who has been called from a neighboring
station to greet his old friend in the ministry, seem tender
and spiritual as words from the other world, and include
supplication for heavenly "protection for the defenders of
our country!"   Full in harmony with the spirit of the occasion is the voice which, resembling still the song of
Marion Belmont of yore, gives, when the veteran has read,
the happy measures of the hymn,

> "O, day of joy and gladness,
>   O, day of rest and balm!"

that, fit for the time and place, contrast how strangely with
the scene from which the warriors have come!   With
breathless interest the people hang on the words of their
faithful friend and minister, as, clad in the garb of war, he
speaks in the church dedicated to the Christ of the gospel
of love, his "faith that the armies of the Union will win
victories that will bring the country peace and establish
the freedom of a race that has been declared by the great
and good Abraham Lincoln!"

Dayville people had just been favored with an early
mail, and when his guest came down to breakfast on Mon-
day morning, Mr. Taylor presented him a letter in which
Colonel Harrison rallied him on being the victim of a
surprise, and asked him to accept, as a token of comradeship, a check for two hundred dollars, with which to purchase blade and uniform befitting his rank.

CHAPTER XII.

ON the evening of his arrival there came to Chaplain Peters a voice within which he at once heeded, a command to pray for—David Grout! Excusing himself, he left the scene of the mating of his two friends and of the heavenly recognition of the fact that had such high significance for them and for him, and, without asking the reason for the command, sought the chamber that had so often been to him the gate of heaven. A contrast, surely, between the home wherein he rejoiced and wherein he was told to pray and the Garden in which, of an evening, centuries before, in agony prayed the Christ. But if this disciple of the Master now thought of that other intercession, as often he did, he stopped not to meditate the difference between the two places of supplication, so quick was he to heed the mandate spoken to his spirit. Bowing, he prayed for blessings on the one, who, of all men in the regiment, was least deserving of any good, prayed with all the faith he could summon when thinking of the tyranny of the man for whom he pleaded. Came there a voice suggesting resemblances as well as contrasts? One of the Twelve of the Petitioner at Gethsemane was a traitor! Did this later day and faithful disciple of the Master think there might be a traitor in the band to which he belonged? There was one in the Thirteenth, who, in a world where every one should be kind, or at least just, to his fellow men, could tyrannize over a boy to whom kindness from him was only justice, one who, to gratify the grudge he had carried from civil life into his army experiences, could tyrannize over his former victim, when serving in the ranks, where he was without power to resent the indignity.

And this cowardly and cruel one could be, on the occasion of sufficient inducement appealing either to the greed for power of which a tyrant is always possessed, the greed for pelf which he often has, or the desire for revenge which he is likely to have—this one, thus false to his obligations to humanity, could be false enough to his obligations to his country to betray her defenders. A tyrant can be a traitor! A tyrant *is* a traitor to those over whom, fearing him, he tyrannizes. And he only needs the opportunity, to betray those over whom, because they do not fear him, he cannot tyrannize. The tyrannical master of one boy can betray a thousand men!—and his country!

Came there to the minister the words from the scriptural account of the scene at Gethsemane, "Rise up, now?" He sought his couch, saying, "I leave him with Thee, O, Lord." In the morning he remembered again the object of his pleading, and, though revealing not the fact of his agony, he was burdened in spirit through the Sabbath of joy.

"Thunder and Mars! Jake, who's the Judis Scarritt of the Thutteenth!"

Sam Biggs and Jake Andrews, whilom acquaintances
of Bill Jones, were such good soldiers that they had each
been twice tendered a sergeant's warrant, which, for some
reason, they declined. So much were they liked that they
were generally granted their request that the two should
be detailed for duty together. Hence the pleasant sobri-
quet of "The Pair," by which they were known. Two of
the sentinels on the picket post nearest the enemy, they
paced the path in front of the picket hut, "torked over "·
old times and touched on "thet air Ath'ton, 'ventor, who
wuz killed by a hoss runnin' erway, that wuz skeered by a
paper flung aout uv the store tew the centre." As the two
"about faced," Jake said, "Sam, there's a piece o' white
paper aout thar whar the folks drives up from daown ken-
try, across the pike leadin' tew Richmun."

"Yis, I seen it, Jake,—what on't? Ef it skeered a hoss
he'd only kill the pesky butternuts thet he wuz a-drorin'—
'n' th' more on 'em the better."

"Sposin' "t'was Ole man Jim Porter, the Unionist, that
was killed?"

"Yer right, Jake, an' suthin' like Elder Peters's 'leadin's'
uv the sperrit' tells me tew git thet air paper tew onst."

It was on Sam's return that he uttered the explosive
above quoted and continued, "By mighty, Jake, treason!
Betrayin' the Thuttenth tew the rebels! Yis, yer see this
ere pass thet one uv ole Grout's men had yisterday, to visit
the York State fellers, he give tew me, an' the ritin' uv one
dockeymunt is just like that of 'tother! Both uv these

dockeymuntz aforesaid, Jake, was rited by thet air Dave Grout aforesaid! An', Jake, the kunnel must hear uv this tew onst! Jake, will you go 'n' tell 'im?'"

"Yis, Sam Biggs, Jake Andrews is jest yer man. Call up Fred Sloan thet's sleepin' in the bunk, so's't there'll be tew tew keep their eyes aout fer ole Grout, who's orsifer uv the day—sposin', Sam Biggs twuz his last time!"

Jake Andrews knew the the sentinel on post at heaquarters, who, as the former gave him the countersign, adding, "I'll bet there's fun ahead for thet air Graout—but mum's the word," whispered, "I never go back on one o' the pair."

Colonel Harrison's face was first pale and then red with indignation on hearing the news divulged by Andrews. He readily believed it, and with a firm step he walked with his adjutant to the quarters of the camp guard where he found Captain Grout, who was enjoining the lieutenant of the detail to see that the "sentinels around the camp are all alert," and saying that he would "visit the pickets, to see that they are watchful,"—after which he would flee to the rebel camp—when Harrison's voice that could be, and naturally was, musical, spoke thus in iron tones:—

"Captain Grout, you are under arrest!" Turning to Jameson, he said, "Adjutant, three trusty men to guard Grout in his quarters—if he moves, shoot him on the spot!"

Each first sergeant noiselessly awoke the men of his company, whispering to each one, "Fall in at once and without a lisp." In ten minutes Harrison's regiment accompanied by another and followed by Major Tompkins and Lieutenant Clinton at the head of a squadron of cavalry, was in motion towards a camp of three regiments of the enemy, to whom, as appeared by the paper discovered, Grout had betrayed his regiment. He had evidently dropped the document the day before, and, strange to say, had not missed it until, in his own quarters he searched his pockets in vain, when, as the guards noticed, he turned pale.

Surprised in the rear by the furious horsemen of Tompkins and Clinton, the rebels, who were about to start to capture the betrayed federals, found two regiments of their expected victims with bristling bayonets in front of them, to whom, after a brief resistance, they surrendered. An hour later they were outside the camp of the Thirteenth, where, guarded, they awaited a trip to a northern prison. Harrison, accompanied by Jameson, called on Grout and, holding before him a missive taken from the rebel leader and the duplicate which had been discovered by "the pair," said, " This letter giving the easiest route of approach to this camp, the number of men reported for duty and the best time for capturing the command, this letter, sir, and the copy discovered by the sentinels, were written by you! I leave you to your reflections!"

In an investigation by fair-minded men of the case against Captain Grout for treason there could have been but one result. And the findings of the general court-martial were in accordance with the facts above recounted.

The evidence showed that the enemy who had suffered great losses at the hands of the Thirteenth thought it best to capture by foul means those whom they could not conquer by honorable warfare. By means of the ubiquitous Simpkins who had again turned up as camp-follower of Harrison's regiment, and had succeeded in eluding the watchfulness of even the vigilant sentinels of that band, they had learned of the jealousy and revengeful feelings of Grout. With him they arranged the betrayal of the regiment, by whom, in striking contrast to their expectations they were captured, while Grout was a prisoner in the hands of those whom he had betrayed! The wily Simpkins had fled the rebel camp as he heard the approach of the federals, repeating, thus, a feat by which he saved himself at the time of his experience as go-between for Phil Pinckney.

Harrison, who, the day after the discovery of Grout's plot, assumed command of the brigade, was visited by the only officer whom the traitor could interest in his own behalf. Summoning Grout, Harrison heard his plea, and gave this fit response: "Sir, it is they who have been kind, they who have been brave, they who have been true, that may ask leinency when overtaken in a fault! But when were you true, or brave, or kind? Thou, tyrant always, and coward, at Gettysburg, at Antietam, and everywhere!

'When wert thou known the ambushed fights to dare,
  Or nobly face the horrid front of war?'

Appeal, sir, if you choose."

At division headquarters General Edgerley soliloquized : " False !—but I pity and will try to save the wretch! " The next day, at Washington, Mr. Lincoln heard him and replied, " No, Edgerley, I like your humanity, but I cannot overlook the perfidy of the man ! " Then, in that vein of humor that gave the president relief from the great cares that burdened him, he proposed that the officer should " measure " with him ; and, this done, the Illinoisan, taking the hand of the Yankee general, exclaimed, as he added another palm to the grasp, " Edgerley, you are nearly as tall as I am, and I believe you are brave enough to deserve the stars you have won."

On his return, the gigantic Edgerley, trembling with emotion and his mild blue eyes filling with tears, said, as he called on the condemned man, " Captain Grout, there is no hope ; and with all my heart I pity you, yes, Captain Grout, I do ! "

Again the chaplain hears and heeds a voice within! Cutting short the much needed furlough that he is enjoying with his friends he hastens to Washington, where, his errand done, he is told by the great and good man who alone can save the traitor :—

" Chaplain, I like your earnestness, your philosophy and your humanity ; but, as I told General Edgerley, I cannot overlook the treason of Grout."

More urging by Peters, and there chanced in the execu-

tive chamber Mr. Lincoln's friend and adviser, the great
New Light divine, Matthew Simpson, who, greeted the
chaplain cordially, when Lincoln said, "Simpson, do you
know him?   What do you think of his errand?"

The bishop listened as the chaplain stated the object
of his errand, when the former said, "Mr. President, from
what I have learned of the results up in New England of
the practice of the chaplain's philosophy of forgiveness,
I am led to think that if you grant the commutation of
sentence which he asks, you will see that your action is
not only humane but wise?"

"I've taken your advice before, bishop, and always
with good results," said Mr. Lincoln, who, taking his
watch, continued, as he turned to the other minister,
"There's just time to save the man."   And he pencils a
message!

It is for the general commanding the army that includes
the Thirteenth, and that, ranged on three sides of a square,
waits in breathless silence some dread denouement!   One
with pinioned arms and attended by a chaplain makes the
rounds of the square, when the minister prays Heaven for
mercy on the pale and trembling man—David Grout!
More than any others to pity the wretch in his trouble and
to despise him for his crime are the soldiers of the regiment he betrayed, but the sight of whose faces intensifies
his punishment?   Not a zephyr fans the trees bordering
the dreadful plain of execution, nor kisses the flowers and
grasses on the hill that overlooks it!   No bird of joy

carols above it! The stillness is condensed to deeper silence and a sense of horror sickens and oppresses be-yond tears even the most hardened of the soldiery. The minister has spoken his last words to the condemned, and tearfully bade him farewell. Thirty paces away, with bowed head, and folded arms, and face of ashy paleness, he stands praying silently but earnestly for the wretched man, who, seated on a coffin facing a firing party of six-teen, awaits his doom! The officer of the guard walks tremblingly but firmly to the prisoner, binds his feet, and draws the black cap over his head! Then, pacing back to the left of his marksmen, he halts facing the general, to whom he lifts his sword in salute. At the commander's nod, he faces about, and to the executioners, who, with effort hold themselves from quivering at thought of the dread work before them, speaks the words—" Make ready! Take aim!"—and the muskets from the eyes of the sixteen gleam straight toward the miserable man! A horseman flying towards the army that awaits dumb with horror at the awful scene to be enacted, pushes into the square and hands a message to the general, who with one glance at the paper spurs his horse forward to the leveled guns and commands, " Recover arms!"

The order of the president changed the sentence from shooting, to dismissal from the army. And, swordless and minus the insignia of his rank, the tyrant and traitor leaves the camp of the regiment he had betrayed. The train by

which he travels northward halts at a station by the side of
one southward bound, and Grout's eyes rest on the eagles
of an officer sitting at the window opposite, and who,
thinking the other may be in need of food, proffers him
a lunch from the well filled basket provided by Mrs. Smith,
who, with her daughter, accompanies him.   The spite of
the wretched man is stronger than his hunger and he
dashes the gift to the ground, muttering as the trains move
apart, "D—n him! The upstart of a New Light! G—d
d—n him , the reprobate !"   David Grout, once, and still,
deacon of the Hardland church of the standing order—
strange for him to curse?   Would not he whose professed
piety did not keep him from the tyranny that was akin to,
and led to, his treason against his country, would not he
hate her defenders enough to curse them?   And would not
he who could be unkind to one of the little ones that were
loved by the Christ be irreverent enough to God to take
His name in vain?"

Mrs. Smith and Agnes bade Colonel Atherton good-bye
at Philadelphia, whence he journeyed southward, they
going to Cohecton, to visit the Slaytons and Miss Ten
Eyck.

CHAPTER XIII.

WELCOME.

WITH the example of the sincere and humble man, Elder Peters, so long before him, Edward Atherton naturally became imbued with a similar spirit. It prompted every act and breathed in every utterance, and all his command remarked how meekly he wore the honors he had so worthily won. Often did the young officer and the veteran minister meet at headquarters or in the chaplain's tent to petition His favor who rules the armies of the world. And for the habit which gained for him the name of "the praying colonel" he was highly respected by officers and men.

At the head of the Thirteenth, recruited to full ranks, and with Frank Dawson as adjutant, he won in the Shenandoah campaigns the thanks of "fighting Phil," whom he equaled in bravery, and received from Washington a commission entitling him to wear a star—to which more success added another. Stedman succeeded to the command of the regiment, which was included in Atherton's brigade and in his division as he was promoted, an arrangement that, to the liking of each, gave Chaplain Peters and Atherton opportunity for frequent meeting. Stedman was soon promoted, when the command of the regiment went to Captain Newton, who wore the eagles well but not long, for he fell in the Wilderness. The decimated

ten companies, gathered into six, were commanded by
Major Frank Dawson, whose adjutant was Fred Sloan,
with Jake Sanders, color-bearer since Gettysburg, carrying
the banner still, and Mike Tobin among the file-closers
of the color company, and, so, near the flag once borne by
his "own dacint Bill Joanes," and "the pair," Biggs and
Andrews, promoted to the color-guard for the vigilance
that circumvented the treasonable plot of Grout. Major
Dawson led the Thirteenth to Appomattox and the grand
Review at Washington. Then, brief guard duty around
the capital in the time of terror following the assassination
of the President. And when, to cheer the patriotic people of Wayfield and Dayville in their mourning at the loss
of the great and loved Lincoln, the May blooms of all
the pleasant hills of the region breathed their balm, and
robins caroled their sweetest notes, and brooks sang in
glad accord, homeward came the war-worn soldiers.

General Harrison, General Edgerley, General Atherton
and General Stedman, had each arranged his army ac-
counts at Washington in season to reach Wayfield by the
same train that bore the Thirteenth, and they were accompanied by Harrison's old adjutant Jameson, who, with his
chief's promotions that entitled him to wear two stars, had
risen, as his first of staff, to the rank of colonel. The
largest hall at Wayfield was the auditorium of the ancient
church, and it was thought none too sacred for the occasion of the welcome proposed for the returned warriors.
Thither thronged the people of the old town and of all

the country for a dozen miles around, to greet and honor the heroes.

They are met by a deputation of fifty citizens at the railway station, where a procession of escort and guests is formed under the direction of Captain Morley, to move through the designated route of march to the place of meeting. He was chosen sheriff of the county the fall previous, with a special sheriff to occupy the place till he should return from the war, and he came on a few days in advance of the regiment to assume the functions of the office, and is by common consent the master of ceremonies of the day of welcome for his comrades and himself. He rides in advance of the column, preceded by mounted police and followed by a band, after which come the citizens, at the head of whom walks Reverend Doctor Robinson and Mr. Payson Sherwood. Next, the fine form of Andrew M. Harrison, first commander of the regiment, and now starred with the insignia of the rank of major-general, which dignity he has acquired by his prowess against the foe, by his humanity, and by the unmilitary and manly recognition of an orphan boy, who, a private in the ranks, so honored the one who honored him as to earn his way to the stars that entitle him now to ride by the side of his benefactor in the triumphal march. The steeds of the officers have been sent in advance of the regiment, and Wildwind seems prouder than ever he did of the chieftain he bears. Thunderbolt, who has carried his young master since his promotion from the line, obeys quickly the gentlest touch of the rein, fierce charger though he is, and taking to the din and carnage of war as naturally as the herd to the hill-side pasture. Following next, are the giant warriors Edgerley and Stedman, whose steeds are proportioned to their burdens and proud of them. Then the beautiful bay of the lamented Newton, led by a groom, walks riderless, while from the pommel of the saddle depends the broken blade yet stained with the blood of the foe whom Newton smote ere he fell! Major Dawson, in immediate charge of the battalion, is at its head, with Adjutant Sloan on his left, and on his right Chaplain Peters. The meeting of the latter and his Billy at the station was affecting in the extreme, the horse rubbing his nose against the face of the preacher with genuine equine love, and the minister leaning on the horse's neck and sobbing with joy. They had met when the chaplain was home on his furlough,—only once in four years. As the column turns from the depot street into Morley, the eyes of the soldiers are greeted on every hand by the national colors that float all along the line of march, inscribed with such words as, "Wayfield welcomes Her Own!" "All Hail to Harrison and his Braves!" "Heaven bless the Warriors who Won!" with a profusion of similar sentiments farther on the way, while floral arches frequently span the route.

Fit is it, that the people and their defenders should be joyous, and the musicians of the town, called into requisition for the occasion, blend their strains with the music of the drum and fife of the regiment through the lively

measures of "When Johnny Comes Marching Home,"
"Yankee Doodle," and "The Girl I Left Behind Me,"
while the nobler melodies of the "Star-Spangled Banner"
express the culmination of the patriotism and joy.

Is there need of mentioning the names of the group in
the grounds of a residence in Morley street, in passing
which generals and officers of every rank lift hats or
blades in token of respect? From the keeping of one of
the women glides a boy exclaiming, "Papa, papa!" The
procession halts, and fearless of harm, the child climbs
with his father's help, from foot to knee and to his embrace! Then is heard, "Yes, Johnny, you may," and from
one clad in widow's weeds a boy of eight runs out and,
taking the hand of General Atherton, springs to a place
in front of the warrior, who says, "Ah, my boy, I knew
your father, Captain Sherwood!" The procession moves
on to the church. Here General Atherton, riding to the side
and head of the line, draws his sword and commands, as
the escort of citizens take their places on either hand of
the entrance, "Column, halt!" Then, at his word, "Column, forward!" the soldiers of the cause of freedom,
under festooning of stars and stripes, enter the house dedicated to the promulgation of the gospel of peace. Doctor Robinson presides, and with him in the ample pulpit
are several officers, including Chaplain Peters, and the
minister of every congregation in the great town, while
before him are the bronzed soldiers, and there, in their garb
of mourning, are the widows of ten of the slain of the

band, one of whom is so crushed by her grief as to leave
not a trace of the joyousness native with the Mary Sumner of other years, while near her, in another pew, sits one
who, in reply to the question of a manly, black-haired boy
by her side, says, " Yes, Teddy, go and sit with Mrs. Newton and Sumner.   It will do her good to have you comfort
the boy—Teddy, just like your father, how I love you!"
After a brief prayer by Doctor Robinson, comes the address of welcome by Mr. Sherwood :—

" Heroes of the gallant Thirteenth!   From the scenes of so much
that was terrible, wherein you did so much that was valorous and suffered with so much fortitude the hardships of war, and wherein so
many of your comrades fell in battle, wasted away by disease, or pined
to death in prison, you have come to receive the greeting of a grateful
people whose homes your heroism has done its full share to defend
and preserve, whose country with its institutions you and others of
like bravery have redeemed from the peril into which it was brought
by traitors, and whose starry flag you and the companion thousands
have given new lustre of honor among the ensigns of the nations of
earth and made it more than ever the emblem of liberty to all mankind !
Ye who come from Spottsylvania, and Yorktown, and Petersburg,
and Chancellorsville, and Antietam, and Gettysburg, and Culpepper,
and Fredericksburg, and Winchester, and the Wilderness, and Appomattox! a message which the lightning of the wires has forwarded
to this meeting tenders the Thirteenth the greeting and the thanks of
His Excellency, the governor, and of the people of the commonwealth.
And hearts that love you bid you welcome to Ridgeway, and Dayville,
and this fine old town of Wayfield, places that are endeared to you by
associations of childhood and boyhood, and from which, in the strength
of young manhood, you went forth to the wars !   Welcome to these
lovely valleys on which the sun shines with new brightness of benediction and to these hills whose brooks and whose birds make sweeter

music than ever before, these valleys and these hills that seem more than ever the fit haunts of the protecting genii of Liberty!

Welcome one and all—Harrison, orator and soldier, mighty on the field of battle as well as convincing at the bar and eloquent on the platform; Jameson, fitted to be adjutant of a thousand or chief-of-staff for the commander of many thousand; Stedman, giant warrior, glad to devote his strength to the defence of the old flag; Edgerley, more gigantic still, the mighty man who single-handed could hew his way through the serried ranks of the foe, but whose blue eyes would melt with pity at thought of the doom awaiting a wrong-doer; Morley, who deemed the ancient name of his family insignificant honor in comparison with the privilege of warring for the flag he loved; and, youngest of them all and excelled in bravery by none, Edward Atherton, the boy soldier, lieutenant, colonel, and general! And welcome Elder John Peters, the veteran of the veterans, whose example of correct life in the army was a constant inspiration to his comrades-in-arms to be as good as they were valiant, and who was so in favor with Heaven as to be given from on high messages, by the heeding of which himself and his band averted danger and won victories that made them a terror to the foe! Aye, welcome, a thousand times welcome, ye war-worn five hundred who remain of the two thousand that, four years ago and at the times of the recruiting of the ranks since then, went forth in their country's service. Welcome survivors of that heroic band, that immortal legion, the invincible Thirteenth! for whom we bespeak and predict the gratitude and the admiration of your countrymen through all time and ask the protection of the ministrants from that other country, who have there welcomed your comrades before you! And welcome here, ye hovering spirits of those who have gone in the advance guard!—the excellent Newton, commander of a company and then wearer of the eagles at the head of the battalion, and whose horse, fitly in the procession to-day, has been riderless since the Wilderness; and the trusty and brave color-bearer, Sergeant William Jones, who though defended with such remarkable bravery by his comrade Tobin, fell at Gettysburg and dying, held aloft the flag, whispering to one who bent beside him, 'Tell Mollie that I love her and be sure you keep the old flag flying!' In remembrance of these words

his comrade Jake Saunders bravely bore the flag and now brings it
home in triumph.   Dear battle-rent ensign, reddened by the blood of
a thousand patriots! with what emphasis thou speakest lessons of
liberty for all mankind and of loyalty to the best government on earth!

And welcome thou spirit of the brave Walbridge, another of the
heroes of Gettysburg, and—for I must speak here the name of my
son—welcome, spirit of Captain Sherwood, whose life he counted
not, and I count not, too dear to give in the country's cause!   And
welcome to the brave and tuneful Captain Theodore Cushman,
descendant of Revolutionary ancestors who fought with Putnam at
Bunker Hill, and with Anthony Wayne at Stony Point, and who suffered with Washington the rigors of the winter in Valley Forge!
Welcome, sweet soul of the brave man who left hymning the praises
in Zion to endure the discord of war and pour out his life blood for
his country!   And Thompson, and Merwin, and others who, through
the dread ordeal of Andersonville passed to the heavenly reward of
their patriotism!   how shall we 'struggle with the emotions that arise
at the mention of your names!'   Fit are ye and all your compatriots
to be chronicled with the bravest of those whose deeds brighten the
pages of history!   Fit are ye to be named with the godlike Wallace,
the Bruce of Bannockburn, and those who erst ascended from the

> 'Land where the gallant Spartan few
>   Bled at Thermopylae of yore!'

Aye, tell me,

> 'Departed spirits of the mighty dead!
>   Ye that Marathon and Leuctra bled!'

tell me, if in the serene heights of the Elysium for the brave, where
ye have been habitants since the days hallowed by your patriotism on
earth, tell me if, since then, there have been admitted to your companionship any nobler than they whose spirits ye have welcomed from
the scenes where they warred and died to uphold the standard of the
Thirteenth in the strife for the cause of good government, American
liberty, and the freedom of mankind! and in their death were fellow
martyrs with the illustrious Lincoln, whose untimely death has bereaved America and the world!

Brave defenders of your country and ours, once more we welcome you to civil life and the congenial pursuits of peace! And we shall ever think ourselves honored to know that you are our fellow citizens in the country wrested of yore from an oppressive monarchy, and by you now saved from destruction plotted by traitors! In strange and pleasant contrast to the hard fare of the camp, a rich and abundant feast has been spread in the town hall, by the women of Wayfield and their sisters from a hundred homes in other towns. To this bountiful board you are invited. And specially fit is it to ask the veteran Chaplain Peters to say grace at this repast and to voice the thanks of us all to Heaven that so many of our loved ones have been returned, and that they who come not back died so nobly for the common cause. Culled from gardens and hillsides, a profusion of flowers shed fragrance to delight you on this day which your patriotism has made joyous and memorable! And supplementing the feast, the inspiring singer, Mrs. Jameson, tuneful as the Marion Belmont she was in the choir of the ancient Dayville meeting-house, will give to the strains of " Hail to the Chief," stanzas penned for this occasion by the gifted Warren, whose poetic soul delights in theme so noble as the patriotism that has made your band immortal!

And, now, heroes, for you no more the lonely vigils of the outpost! No more fatiguing marches over the rough, and miry, and dusty roads, through drenching rain or glaring sun! No more the bivouac on the hard, cold earth, amid the chill damps of the night! No more camping in the miasmatic swamps of death! No more the rattle of musketry, the roar of cannon, the shock of contending armies! the indescribable carnage of war! Instead, welcome, a thousand times welcome to the comforts and joys of home, the blessings of peace, the benedictions of a grateful people, and the admiration of the world!"

In his response, voicing the joy of his companions-in-arms, at seeing home once more and their gratitude for the greeting accorded them, General Harrison, thanked them, "officers and men, and brothers all, whatever the rank that either held," for what they had done " to make successful the country's cause and to give the Thirteenth a fame lustrous as the stars!" Then, in the eloquence of tender regard and profound admiration, he referred to the "slain warriors of the band" and closed with this apostrophe to the martyred president:—

"That most terrible taking off, that has darkened the pages of history! that most mysterious of the dispensations of the gods in all time, that has come to sadden the American people in these days of their rejoicing over the victories and the peace their noble armies have won!—tell me, Socrates, looking from thy serene height, tell me, thou sage, if ever a wiser one was admitted to thine exalted companionship than the great American leader whom thou hast welcomed to the rewards of the knowing and the good! And tell me, thou ascended Father of thy country, was ever man more patriotic on earth than was he, the Savior of his country, whom thou hast welcomed to thy fellowship in the 'land of the leal,' the heroic and true! Tell me, O, ye of all time, whose patience under wrong, whose forbearance with the erring, whose forgiveness of enemies, whose blessing those that slew, have given bliss above,—was there ever greater, nobler, purer, completer unselfishness than that exhibited in the life and death of him whom ye have latest honored yourselves by welcoming on high! Tell me, ye clearest visioned of the translated seers, was there ever among the bards of earth, one who kenned and spoke sublimer truth than did this one in his matchless words at Gettysburg! Tell me, O, all ye benefactors of mankind, who have risen to the rewards of Elysium,—who among you so great, so incomparably good as the Savior of the American Republic! the emancipator of a race! the immortal Abraham Lincoln!"

Feasting, singing and good-byes at Wayfield over, with an occasion of similar joyousness the next day at Dayville, the regiment re-assembled a week later to be mustered out of service, when good-byes again, and—the Thirteenth passed into history!

As on the return of the anniversary of Gettysburg or of
others of the engagements that made possible the glorious
significance of Appomattox, the veterans recount the campaigns of the regiment to their children and children's
children, they will shed tears of "exultation, of gratitude
and of joy" that they were members of the old Thirteenth! And so the dear memories clustering around the
name of the gallant legion shall brighten as the years
come and go in the progress of the country which the
band did so much to rescue from peril and re-establish
among the nations of the earth!

CHAPTER XIV.

Weddings, Dedications and Christenings.

TO those whose souls have mated and whose vows have been witnessed by angels and written in heaven, of little consequence comparatively is the ceremony making their nuptials legal on earth. Yet, as such rite was an event in the lives of Edward Atherton and Agnes Graham Smith, let it be here recorded that the words rendering their marriage valid according to the enactments of men were spoken by their friend Elder Peters, when, soon after the heroes of the Thirteenth came from the wars, the June roses perfumed the airs melodious with the bird-songs of peace and joy! To hear his declaration of their union and his benediction on their lives, the two stood amid a profusion of flowers in the place where the devout had so often kneeled to pray and lingered to receive the answers of peace that were ever sure to come, and where the two heard the sanction of their mating spoken from the skies.

When there came a pause in the congratulations Doctor Robinson announced and read, "Reverend Wilbur F. Warren's fine rhythmic tribute to the wedded." And, thronging through the house at the general reception that now followed, a thousand people of Dayville and Wayfield took the hands of the Athertons and inspected the array of gifts bestowed by five hundred of them and speaking

the good will of all. Visiting the grounds to discuss the
feast of choice viands burdening long tables improvised
for the occasion, and made fragrant and beautiful with
roses of the choicest perfume,—bestowed, it need not be
said, by the father of the bride,—the company learned of
another feature of the joyousness of the day, when General Harrison asked their attention as he treated "his
friend and everybody's friend, General Atherton, to a surprise different from those which he so often enabled the
first colonel of the Thirteenth to give the foe in the field,
who found to his sorrow that the second colonel fully
equaled his predecessor in daring and the capacity for
strategy. For," continued Harrison, "I have to say that,
warranted by evidence enough to convince the most stub-
born jury and the most adversely prejudiced judge, that
Lemuel Barnes had no right to the income from the inventions of the late Edward Atherton, and that the income
belonged to the inventor's son, namesake and heir, Colonel Jameson brought a suit against Barnes for two hundred and fifty thousand dollars, in behalf of General Atherton, attached every iota of the defendant's estate, and
compelled Barnes to settle for the full amount, plus ample
fees for the counsel and senior counsel retained in behalf
of the plaintiff. And papers transferring to Atherton a
bank account of fifty thousand dollars, with government
bonds, shares of the Wayfield railroad corporation, and
other securities to the amount of the *ad damnum* and fees,
were signed by the defendant on the spot, the schedule

of property made over, including, also, several valuable pieces of land and, in the poetic justice of the proceedings, the little brown house by the roadside where the inventor lived with his son. I join with you, ladies and gentlemen, in congratulating the recipient of this deserved good fortune and in wishing him and his joy on the journey of life."

In his reply, General Atherton said :—

"My friends, this is indeed a day of joy for me. My foster parents, the Taylors, made the sunrise memorable by awakening me to read a document, transferring to me a half interest in the property and business of Taylor's mills. And the income from this, with the savings from my salary as an army officer, will be enough for a living, and the fortune with the possession of which I have been surprised I shall devote largely to objects that will benefit the town and perpetuate the name of my father—fifty thousand dollars towards the fund for the house of worship which the New Lights need, one hundred thousand to found the Atherton Academy, and the remainder for purposes to be named hereafter. Thanking my many good friends in Dayville and Wayfield for the interest they have manifested in my welfare from the day when I was rescued to this time which they have made so glad, and recognizing Him whose hand has led the fatherless through the most trying vicissitudes to this hour of high happiness, I commend you with all your interests to the Gracious One, whose blessing I invoke for myself and mine."

The site selected for the Atherton Academy was an eminence in the northern part of the town which commanded a view of a wide extent of country. The edifice, made of granite from the quarry on the Hardland road, was completed in the spring of 1866, and arbutus blooms shed fragrance from the desk of the academy hall where Elder Peters pronounced his fit words of dedication, in conclusion proclaiming, "Grace, grace unto it!"

When next came the efflorescence of June, the New Lights had completed a fine church building with auditorium containing thrice the number of sittings of the one it had displaced, and with the pulpit directly over the spot of the pulpit of the other, and, so, where stood the desk of the school-house on which sixteen years before a vase of plain flowers was placed by a child, who was encouraged by her mother to act according to her own bright idea of the adornment. She was not present at the ceremony of consecrating the new sanctuary, but the vase was still in existence, treasured by her. mother, who lent it to Mrs. Jameson for the day. And, filled with marigolds and sweet-williams from the same garden where those grew in the other June, it was given the place of honor in the array of roses, lilies, laurels and ferns that graced the pulpit and altar. Supplementing the matchless address of dedication by the great divine of the New Lights, Matthew Simpson, that had fitting accompaniment of song by Mrs. Jameson and others, there was a ceremony wherein Elder Peters officiated, assisted by the orator of the day, and in

which those especially interested were General Thomas
Stedman and Lillie J. Ten Eyck. The benediction of the
bishop was followed by a scene of congratulations wherein
the first participants were Hannah Slayton Gray and the
medical gentleman who, since the scene of an August
morning in 1863, had induced the Quakeress to add a
name to hers. And beautifully quaint was the initial
greeting of them all by the woman from Cohecton, "Thee
has done well, Lillie, and so has Thomas."

General Harrison had, in and out of army life, originated, or participated in, so much that was unexpected,
exceeding so often the hopes of his associates and his
friends and the fears and even the surmises of his opponents, that it had come to be supposed that when he rose
in public to speak, a revelation awaited his hearers. And
when, from the open in front of the pulpit, he asked the
attention of the concourse, there was silence at once.
Murmurs of applause greeted the paper which he read
announcing the gift of fifteen thousand dollars by Mrs.
Stedman, which had reverted to her from the "Creek-side"
estate of her father, in New York, and which she proposed
to devote to completing the payment of the cost of the
new church. But a surprise was now in store which exceeded any that Harrison had ever made and that would
cause more joy than them all. "This legacy," continued he,
"leaves unpaid of the cost of the church and furnishing,
the sum of one thousand dollars, which is due on the
organ, and this I gladly pay as a compliment to my New

Light friends and as a thank-offering to the One who has so long and so kindly led me when I knew it not. Yes, my friends, I note the look of mingled joy and wonder on the faces before me. But the unbeliever has come to see that there is a God, and asking the forgiveness of the Benignity for the doubt and ingratitude of the past, he announces, here and now, his allegiance to the Christian faith, and his gratitude to the Father for all the blessings that crown his days! Whatever talent may have been given him, and whatever health vouchsafed, was bestowed by the hand of the All-Gracious, by whose protection alone he came safe through the dangers of four years of campaigning in the country's cause. And only by Heaven's blessing on the bravery of its defenders is that country reunited, prosperous, and, more than any other nation, the ideal of the peoples of earth! Leading to the conclusion to which I have come are several reasons other than those here stated, which I have rehearsed in full to that one who is more interested in this experience of mine than is, or can be, any one other than myself. But one of those reasons it seems fitting to state here, as I do in referring to the unobtrusive piety and consistent life of Elder Peters, whose earnestness in the cause in which he is enlisted never led him in the many years of our acquaintance to exceed good taste in promulgating the gospel he believed or inviting people to the standard of the Master whom he loved."

" Rejoicing," said Elder Peters, " in the revelation made,

I wish to take no credit to myself, but, congratulating
General Harrison on the step he has taken, I say, as did
one of old, 'This is the Lord's doing, and it is marvellous
in our eyes!'"

As the veteran preacher and the great divine walked from
the church, the former said, " Brother Simpson, at this hour
of a beautiful June day sixteen years ago, I was called to
officiate at a baptismal ceremony at the house to which we
are going. A little girl who was one of the three persons
then consecrated is now a mother, and you are asked to par-
ticipate with me in the christening of the little one."

Parents, grandparents and other kindred and near
friends were grouped around the two ministers, as Elder
Peters, taking the child from its mother's arms and looking benignly into the brown eyes, repeated the good Scotch
name she pronounced, and said as he placed the crystal
drops on the brow of the wee one, " Ellen, I baptize thee
in the name of the Father, and of the Son, and of the
Holy Ghost. Amen."

"The Lord bless the dear child and those to whom she '
is given—at once their joy and their care, their hope and
their responsibility!"—and the voice of the eloquent
Simpson never sounded sweeter nor more inspiring when
swaying the thousands with the grace and fervor of his
matchless periods than it did in this utterance which closed
the baptismal scene. Ominous may the words be of bright
days for the bairn and for those of whose love she is the
evidence, the blossoming and the fruitage.

"Well, well, my friends," said General Harrison, returning from answering a summons for him at the door of the Smith mansion, after the christening, "if General Edgerley and that bright little jewel of his haven't surprised us all! They've had it planned for weeks that the clergymen officiating at the dedication of the new church should speak the words to make them one—words which, to do them justice, I should say they have for years been ready to hear, and, so, in no hurry to hear. Miss Davis, who was companion of Mrs. Harrison during my campaigning and who since then has remained our welcome guest and friend, we could not prevail upon to come with us to the dedication, and the general was 'absent on important business!' But he returned an hour after Mrs. Harrison and I drove away, and he sends now a note in advance of his coming, requesting the presence of Mr. Peters and his distinguished friend at Edgerley's new house, in the near vicinity of the home of our friends the Smiths, and also asking them, the Athertons, the Taylors, and any whom either family wish to invite,—or, I should say, *can* invite on such short notice,—to attend the pleasant ceremony anticipated. The note also states that General and Mrs. Stedman will be present. And, so, it seems they have been party to the plan of that Edgerley, and I see that, strangest of all, a look on the face of the saintly Peters suggests that he too may have been knowing to the plot of outwitting their old comrade-in-arms. I'll get even with the fellows, yet, for their treachery—see if I don't!"

Towering far above even the tall forms of Stedman and the minister who was to assist Elder Peters in the ceremony, General Timothy Edgerley looked down beyond the benignant face of the divine to the diminutive and delighted one, reaching up to his gigantic hand the palm proportioned to that which grasped it as a lily is to an oak, and, to the words, " Do you take this woman to be your wife," responded " Yes, I do "—an utterance which Elder Peters and General Stedman remembered hearing before, from the same lips, but under far different circumstances. When, in response to a similar question, the tiny woman spoke in clear, tender tones, " I most certainly do," the blue eyes of the giant brimmed with tears of joy and the other minister declared the twain one. The visiting clergyman, driven with business as he ever was, but still driving it rather than being driven by it, remembered an appointment elsewhere for the evening, and the train leaving the Dayville station in thirty minutes would be the last one to take him to his destination in season. But he had a moment to subscribe, with the other minister officiating with him, documents prepared in blank for permanent record of the two marriages of the day. The Edgerleys, who were to include their native Ammonoosuc region and the White Mountains in their tour, were accompanied by the Stedmans, who proposed the mountains and the Maine coast for theirs; and with the party journeyed, for a distance, the great Simpson, who as the trainman called the name of the town where he was to officiate at another dedication, said, with that depth of tenderness of voice which once heard in benediction could never be forgotten, "The Lord give you, my friends, the choicest of heaven's blessings!"

The receptions of the Stedmans and the Edgerleys at their new homes were pleasant events of the midsummer for them and for the people of Dayville, while General Harrison, in pursuance of his threat of retaliation for the "treachery" shown him by the benedicts and Elder Peters, appeared at each joyous scene with a party of fifty Wayfield people headed by the Sherwoods and Robinsons, and on the second evening, the time of greeting the Edgerleys, announced, after a brief "aside" with General Atherton and Mr. Smith, a plan for sending Stedman to the Senate of the state and Edgerley to the House, each for two terms, "after which," said Harrison, "it will be in order—begging pardon for the play upon words—to make the tallest man higher,—a member of the Senate!" The idea took with the people, and "the giants," as their fellow legislators sometimes pleasantly called the two, made a creditable record at the capitol, and the few criticisms that appeared in print against them heightened the estimation in which they were held, when it was found that the strictures were inspired by lobbyists who could not influence them to vote against their convictions.

At the home of the Edgerleys a fine painting of a cascade of a tributary of the Ammonoosuc was hung, the gift of the Jamesons, and subscribed with the artist's autograph, "Evartson," while another work by the same painter, and the gift of the Athertons and the Harrisons, was placed to adorn the house of the Stedmans and remind them of the fine view from the veranda of "Sunnyside" cottage at Cohecton. And facing each picture was a parchment, framed in fit setting of gold, bearing date of a day in June, 1866, and subscribed,

"M. SIMPSON,
JOHN PETERS."